PRAISE F

"The Pameroy mysteries never disappoint! I love how history gets mixed into the present. After reading this book, I really feel like I know Lillia and her Grauntie. Great read. Can't wait for the next!"

"What a fun mystery! I feel like I am right there with Lillia and Charlie during their adventures. Humorous, lighthearted and quite a page turner! I will definitely be recommending this one every chance I get!"

"Drawn into this book right from the beginning! My thirteen-year-old niece has read both books in this series and loved them. So, it's been nice that we've both enjoyed and can chat about them! Great read not just for tweens."

LOCKED DOORS

A PAMEROY MYSTERY

BRENDA FELBER

Locked Doors, A Pameroy Mystery

Cover design eBook Launch/Laughing Deer Press

Publisher's Cataloging-in-Publication data

Names: Felber, Brenda, author.

Title: Locked doors / Brenda Felber.

Series: A Pameroy Mystery

Description: Schofield, WI: Laughing Deer Press, 2017

Identifiers: ISBN 978-0-9909092-6-2 (pbk.) | 978-0-9909092-7-9 (ebook) | LCCN 2017952078

Summary: Lillia doesn't know the sad dark history of the haunted mansion. But when the ghost a of young girl asks her for help, she will soon discover the truth.

Subjects: LCSH Friendship--Juvenile fiction. | Psychics--Juvenile fiction. | Logging--Wisconsin--History--Juvenile fiction. | Lumber trade--Wisconsin--Juvenile fiction. | Family--Juvenile fiction. | Ginseng--Juvenile fiction. | Mystery fiction. | Ghosts--Juvenile fiction. | Ghost stories. | BISAC JUVENILE FICTION / Mysteries & Detective Stories | JUVENILE FICTION / Horror & Ghost Stories | JUVENILE FICTION / Paranormal, Occult & Supernatural

Classification: LCC PZ7.F33375 Lo 2017 | DDC [Fic]--dc23

CONTENTS

QUOTE TO PONDER...

"Youth can not know how age thinks and feels. But old men are guilty if they forget what it was to be young."

J.K. Rowling
    (Harry Potter and the Order of the Phoenix)

1

LILLIA

I rolled down my car window. Moist chilly fog fingers slid across my cheeks. Winds, that had pushed dark clouds ahead of us for the past two hours, stilled.

Large limbs of trees, their trunks thick with age, reached across the curved drive. In the headlight beams, I saw my brother Charlie struggling to push the rusty gate open.

Better get out and help him, or we'll be sitting here all day I thought.

With a glance back at the angry gray clouds hanging suspended overhead, I stopped by the driver side window. "Grauntie, wasn't that guy expecting us? Think he would have had the gates unlocked."

Grauntie Nora shrugged and said, "They might be rusted tight shut. That'll happen to gates if they don't get used. I'll help Charlie too."

I had my doubts about this. If this gate isn't used much, is anyone even waiting for us? Or are we headed for an empty house?

The three of us almost tumbled down on top of each other as the gate finally gave way with a horrible screech.

With an uneasy laugh, Grauntie said, "Teamwork!"

Charlie's eyes were taking in the misty air closing in around us. "Are you sure this is the right place? Maybe we should drive away? Doesn't feel like anyone lives here."

"Or we could go back across that stone bridge and stop at the farm we passed. They might be able to help us," I said, for once agreeing with Charlie's assessment of a situation.

"I'll walk back and check the name on the mailbox across the road," Charlie said.

I felt rain start and ran back to the car. Here we were, in the middle of Wisconsin, with a storm dumping cold water on us. Part of me wanted this to be the place so we could get out of this weather, but the bigger part of me hoped that the name Meyer wasn't on that mailbox and we could leave this creepy place.

Grauntie climbed back in behind the steering wheel. She peered ahead, her white-knuckle grasp on the wheel telling me she wasn't so sure about this either.

Charlie bounded back in the car and shook the rain out of his hair.

"Hey thanks a lot," I said, as the scattering drops hit me.

He shook his wet hair in my direction again. "I couldn't read the name on the mailbox. The letters were worn off."

Grauntie Nora pulled out her cell phone to look at the map again. "I put in the address John gave me, and this is the spot. I could have gotten an address number wrong I guess. Let's drive in and check the place out. With this elaborate of a gate, seems like we've found the entrance to Edgewater Estate."

The wind picked up again, sending trees swaying. Rain hammered on the car's roof as we made our way up the drive.

Suddenly, as the drive took a turn, and through the rain and fog, a dark house appeared in front of us. It was huge, three stories high, with a tall tower rising up above the roof.

2

ARRIVAL AT EDGEWATER ESTATE

Nora's unease grew. Driving up a small rise and turning to follow the curve, she expected to see a grand house. But what appeared in her headlights startled her. The mansion loomed, foreboding. Weeds grew in abandoned flower beds. No lights shone in any of the windows.

Charlie pressed his face against the car window, his breath steaming the inside of the glass. "I don't think anyone lives here Grauntie Nora. Let's go."

Lillia, looking through her open window, said, "What a strange looking tower. I think there is someone up in it. Watching us."

Charlie, wide-eyed, craned his neck to look up at the tower. "Don't tease me Lillia. I don't like this place. I think it wants us to go away."

Nora heard the tremor in Charlie's voice. He's not a

fan of old houses. The gloomy clouds and rain didn't help the mood.

"Don't tease your little brother like that," Grauntie said.

This wasn't what she expected. John mentioned his family had been wealthy at one time, but a gate set in stone piers seemed out of place among the cow pastures and fields of corn. Then seeing this house looking so abandoned and sad, she felt her decision to stay here might have been a mistake.

"What is that tower for anyway?" Charlie asked.

"I'm not sure," Nora said, distracted by her thoughts. "Looks like a bell tower."

She replayed the conversation she'd had with the woman who answered the phone three weeks ago when Nora called. The phone seemed to ring a long time, and she was about to hang up when someone picked up on the other end.

Nora said a cheerful, "Hello?"

No answer, but there was crackling on the line. Maybe a bad connection?

Again, a bit louder she said, "Hello? Is this Walter Meyer?" He might think I'm trying to sell him something, so she quickly added, "I'm a friend of your nephew, John."

BRENDA FELBER

She knew someone was on the line. Louder still, "HELLO? Is someone there?"

Finally, a faraway voice said, "Hello Nora. I apologize for the delay. It took me a moment to find my voice. I am Judith, the head housekeeper."

Hmm, Nora thought, how does she know my name? "Hello, Judith. Is Mr. Meyer there please?"

"Walter is out of doors at this time. Perhaps I can help you?"

"It's rather personal. I'm a friend of Walter's nephew John," Nora said.

Judith said, "Johnny! Oh my, we have not heard from him in years. Walter will be so delighted to receive your call. I would be happy to try to locate him. However, I am afraid he wanders rather far sometimes. Shall I take a message?"

Nora paused, uncertain how much more she should say. "Could Walter return my call when it's convenient?"

"Oh dear, I am afraid that would be difficult. You see Nora, Walter is getting old and has a bit of dementia. Perhaps, it would be better if you leave a message with me. Is Johnny coming for a visit?" Judith asked. A pause, then, "Johnny is well, isn't he?"

Walter must be in his nineties, and it wouldn't do to hear something like this from a stranger. So Nora decided it might be best to tell Judith that John had died and let her convey the sad news to Walter. "Judith, I'm so sorry to tell you this, but John passed away a few months ago."

A soft gasp came through the phone line before Judith replied, "Oh my, I had a feeling it could be bad news."

"John gave me this number for his Wisconsin family. He wants me to return to his old fishing hole on Silver Creek and spread some of his ashes there. He suggested I'd be welcome to stay and visit with his uncle."

"Of course you will be welcome to stay with us. I will prepare a room for you. We have closed up most of the house as Walter is the only Meyer family member living at Edgewater Estate now."

"Oh, that's so kind of you. I'll have my grandniece and grandnephew with me. They'll sleep anywhere. I don't want to be a bother."

"Children in this house again sounds delightful. When do you anticipate arriving?"

"In about three weeks if that works. I thought we'd arrive the night before. He asked me to get in touch with a couple of other old friends he'd like to be at the memorial service as well. To say goodbye to him so to speak."

"I insist you come several days earlier Nora. That will allow time for you to relax and enjoy your visit to John's childhood home. And it will give Walter something to look forward to after I give him the sad news. He will be so happy to have the company."

Nora was glad to hear that. She'd never been to Wisconsin and always loved exploring new locations. "Well, if you're certain, I'll take you up on it. Monday the fifth okay with you?"

"Yes, it is. However, I fear I will not be here to greet you that day. I will be certain that Walter knows to expect you and the children. The front door will be unlocked. Please let yourself in. Walter often wanders or sits out back on the patio. There is a chance he will not hear the knocker," Judith said.

"John left a key marked Edgewater, does that still work?"

Judith chuckled saying, "I rather imagine it does. You will discover that here at Edgewater Estate it is like time stood still! Including no change of locks in decades. And please Nora, patience with Walter. His episodes of forget-fulness and confusion seem to be worsening. Your visit will do him good."

"See you soon then," Nora said.

"Safe travels to you and the children."

Nora had tried calling earlier today to give Judith or Walter an arrival time. No one answered so she left a message.

Did anyone pick up that message?

3

LILLIA

I could tell Grauntie Nora was trying to take it all in and calm Charlie down when she said, "My goodness! Quite the place. Bet she was beautiful in her prime."

Charlie said, "It looks spooky to me. I don't think I want to stay here. Can't we stay at a hotel in that little town we just passed through?"

"Of course not Charlie. We're expected here, and here we are. Let's go up and see if Walter or Judith are home."

We all took shelter under Grauntie's big umbrella to run up under the porch roof. I couldn't find a door bell to push, but Grauntie grabbed a tarnished piece of metal hanging on the door. "I think we have the right place. John's family were wealthy lumbermen and this door knocker is shaped like an ax. Watch this," she said as she clapped it against the metal plate.

No one came to the door.

Charlie shuffled from foot to foot.

"Stop it," I snapped at him. I didn't understand his being creeped out by old houses. I loved them. Always have. But I had to admit there was a different vibe about this place. Not that I'd tell him that.

Grauntie reached for the knocker again, this time hammering it harshly. "Anyone inside will be sure to hear that."

No response.

"Charlie, would you run around to the back and see if anyone is there?" Nora said, then added under her breath, "Though I doubt it on a day like this."

Charlie asked me to come with him, and I jumped at the chance to check out the back. I opened up the umbrella again.

"Lillia, give a holler if you find anyone. Judith said she'd leave it unlocked, so I'll let myself in if no one answers the door soon."

We hadn't even gotten to the corner of the house when Grauntie called for us to come back. She was shaking the hand of a gray-haired old man who had answered the door. He leaned on his cane, listening to Grauntie try to explain who she was. His bewildered expression grew when he saw Charlie and I come running up the porch steps.

"I'm sorry if I'm confusing you. I've spoken with your housekeeper Judith regarding us coming."

"Judith? And you say you know Johnny?" he said in a weak voice.

"Yes, your nephew was a very dear friend of mine. We've known each other for over forty years."

"I haven't seen him in a long time," the man said as he peered around Grauntie to look at Charlie and me. "And who are these two young people?"

Charlie stepped forward and reached out his hand. "I'm Charles Pameroy. We drove all the way from Kansas to visit you."

The man said, "Well now Charles, isn't that something? Kansas is a long way from here."

"This is my older sister Lillia Pameroy."

"Pleasure to meet you both. I'm Mr. Walter Meyer. Please come in and get out of this damp air. We'll figure out what we have going on here."

Grauntie waved us to go ahead of her as she shut the heavy wooden door behind us.

A dusty chandelier hung from the high ceiling of the hall we had entered. Ahead of us, a wide, carpeted staircase rose into the darkness of a second floor. The place was dead quiet except for the creaking floor boards under Charlie's nervous feet. I nudged him to stand still.

Mr. Meyer hesitated and seemed confused as to what to do with us.

We stood staring at each other a few minutes before Grauntie asked, "Is Judith here today?"

"Judith?"

"Your housekeeper," Grauntie said.

"My housekeeper? I don't believe so. Was she supposed to be here?" Uncertain about what was going on, he mumbled a couple more words and then abruptly offered us cookies and milk in the kitchen. "Come this way, follow me. Don't even know if children drink milk anymore, but I figure they still like cookies."

We followed him across the grand entrance hall. Arched openings revealed rooms to each side. Light escaped out past the edges of a door ahead of us. Then, as Mr. Meyer pushed it open, the light spilled into the dim hall, and I walked right into Charlie who had stopped dead in his tracks.

"Lillia, look at that lady's eyes. I think they moved." He pointed to a large portrait hanging near him.

Mr. Meyer said, "That's my grandmother Augusta Meyer. We always said she had eyes in back of her head. The one next to her is of my mother, Stella Meyer."

I stepped up closer to the painting for a good look at the woman's eyes. "Don't be silly Charlie." But as I stepped forward toward the open door, I swear the eyes followed me too. Backed up. They moved. Stepped forward two steps, and again they moved, following me.

Charlie whispered, "See?"

"Just an illusion," I said as I brushed past him.

"Here we go!" Mr. Meyer said. "Now you see why I didn't hear the door knocker sounds at first. Besides my bad hearing, the front door is a good walk away from the kitchen."

The clouds had cleared and weak sunshine found its way in through the kitchen window. Everything seemed to be from another time. Tall cupboards rose up to the ceiling. Stacks of fancy plates and bowls and glasses visible through glass-fronts.

Mr. Meyer was asking, "Where's Johnny again?" as I peeked out the window above the sink. Oh-oh, sounds like he doesn't realize John is dead. Guess Grauntie has some sad news to deliver. Poor old guy.

Grauntie gave me a *what should I say* look as Mr. Meyer pulled back chairs for us to sit around a large wooden table.

He didn't wait for a response to his question about Johnny. Instead, he reached in one of the cupboards for glasses, saying, "Milk for the children. Is coffee okay with you Nora? I brewed some earlier."

Charlie made a *yuck I don't like milk* face at me behind Grauntie's back. I shook my head side to side, the clue for him to stop it. Sometimes twelve-year olds understand things better. I knew we would be forced to accept the milk offered. To be polite. Hope the cookies are at least recognizable.

4

MILK AND COOKIES

After everyone was settled down with their milk, coffee, and cookies, Walter said, "So now. How can I help you?" Walter was glad to have some company. And they seemed very nice he thought. He had been playing their names over and over in his head to remember them. "Oh yes, we were talking about young Johnny."

Nora could tell Walter was tiring. Judith had said he got confused at times. I'll have to pick the right moment to break the news about his nephew's death. To hear that, from a complete stranger who appeared on your doorstep just minutes ago, didn't feel like the best time.

Nora reached over to touch his hand resting on the scarred surface of the sturdy kitchen table. "Walter, you've welcomed us weary travelers with food and drink. We appreciate that."

She gave a little shooing motion with her hands to Lillia and Charlie. "Looks like the sun is peeking out. How about you two go outside and explore the grounds? Is that okay with you Walter?"

Walter looked from Nora to the two children with his pale, watery eyes and smiled. "Oh yes, please. You can head out that door right there."

It didn't take Lillia and Charlie but a minute to put their glasses in the deep white porcelain sink and bolt out the door.

"I'm so sorry we've sprung our visit on you. Must be a bit unsettling to have unexpected visitors show up on your doorstep," Nora said.

Walter said, "I enjoy the company. Gets quite lonely here at times. Please tell me more about my nephew Johnny."

Nora first spoke of John's life in South Dakota, before breaking the news of his death. She talked about how much he had loved the forests and the Black Hills. How he had built and ran the Overlook Resort until just recently.

Walter said, "Sounds like Johnny was a happy man. I love forests too. I worked for many years in the forestry and landscaping field." He stopped, shaking his head, looking confused before continuing, "I should have known about Johnny's passing. Did I tell you I get mixed up? My memory isn't what it used to be."

Nora smiled and said, "My goodness Walter, you just welcomed complete strangers and heard some surprising news. I'd be confused too. I spoke with Judith, and she was going to tell you about John, so it caught me off guard when you didn't know."

Lines crinkled across Walter's forehead before he chuckled and said, "She very well might have told me and I just forgot."

Nora smiled back at him. "I'm grateful you agreed to let us stay with you. If you could show me the room Judith prepared for us, I'll get our suitcases out of the car."

"She has a room ready for you? I'm not sure which one that would be. Let me think," Walter said.

Through the window over the sink, Nora saw Lillia and Charlie outside on the sprawling yard. Maybe Charlie was right, and they should go back and stay at a hotel in town.

"If Judith told you she prepared a room for you then that's what she did. I must have forgotten her mentioning it. Let's go and find it." He pushed himself up from his chair and reached for his cane on the chair's back. Picking up his coffee cup, he shuffled slowly toward the sink.

"Tell you what Walter, if you'll allow me to explore, I'm sure I can find the room myself. I'll bet you're exhausted from entertaining three surprise guests."

Walter turned to look at Nora and nodded. "I think you're right. I am feeling a wee bit tired. I'm often in my robe and slippers by this time, and watching the local news in my bedroom recliner."

"Well then, you head on off to your bedroom. I'll wash up our dishes. It's the least I can do,"

"I haven't kept up with household chores I'm afraid. Became like my grandmother Augusta, just closing and locking doors as rooms were no longer needed. Please feel free to explore. Make yourself at home. The bedrooms are all on the second and third floors."

Nora patted Walter on his thin shoulders. "Thank you. I'll figure it all out. You look tired, so scoot along now, and I'll see you in the morning."

He started down a back hallway that left the kitchen.

"Ah, Walter? Isn't your bedroom upstairs too?" Nora asked.

Walter stopped and looked over his shoulder. "Nope. Got to be too hard on that big staircase for me. My neighbors moved my things in the maid's room down the hall from here. Much easier for me. Goodnight Nora."

"Goodnight Walter," Nora said. "Oh and we're going

to Merrill in the morning. The children and I have a traveling tradition. Our first morning in a new place we have ice cream instead of breakfast. I hope you'll join us."

Walter said, "That sounds like fun. Just might take you up on that. Thank you for asking."

"Goodnight." Second and third-floor bedrooms Nora thought. Goodness, how big is this place? I hope ours are on the second floor.

As she tidied the kitchen, she found herself peeking in some of the many cabinets and pulling open a few of the drawers. Walter was right. It looked like things were left untouched for years. Beautiful china patterns, plates stacked high with matching bowls, saucers, cups, serving pieces. Crystal glasses side by side on wooden shelves. Closer inspection revealing tiny chips in some of the crystal glass edges. Silver utensils, sadly tarnished, lay in the wide, deep drawers.

She could almost hear the bustle of bygone days. Staff preparing dinner. Beats of knives chopping vegetables on the butcher block counter. Clangs of spoons against sides of pans holding simmering sauces on the gas stove. Chatter of maids pushing through the door into the dining room with full platters of meats and tureens of steaming soups.

She peeked down the back hall. A light shone under

one of the doorways. She walked toward it and leaned her ear against the door. The sound of faint television voices let her know he had settled in. Good, now I'd better find our spot to sleep tonight.

5

LILLIA

I watched Charlie race across the patio. He stopped at a low stone wall on the far side. In spite of the messy jumble of old outdoor furniture in the corner and the dozens of dead potted plants, I could tell the patio had been beautiful once. Furniture would have been arranged to enjoy the view at sunset. Hummingbirds and bees would have been fighting over the sweet nectar of bright colored flowers growing in the pots.

The setting sun's rays hit the misty air on the horizon, and a rainbow emerged. Bands of color arced over the forested hills. I took a deep breath, pulling fresh air into my lungs.

I joined Charlie at the edge of the patio. A mountain rose in the distance. And below us lay a softly curving river. The wide, smooth surface held barely a ripple to break the reflections of the trees on its banks and the sky above. "That's got to be the Wisconsin River," Charlie said. "I saw it on the map. It goes all the way to the Mississippi."

He scrambled over the low stone wall. "Bet this was their backyard once. It doesn't look like anybody has cut it in a long time." He kicked his feet along through tall lawn grasses, before throwing himself into the fresh, moist greenery, and rolling down the hill toward the water.

"Charlie, be careful. Might be rocks buried in there."

He popped up and waved, shouting, "Nope it's fine. Come on down. You can see the river better." And with that he threw himself at the earth again, this time doing somersaults.

I couldn't resist climbing over the small wall myself. After being in the car all day and then having to sit and visit with Walter, rolling down a grassy hill sounded like the right thing to do. The grass was wet and slippery from the fog that had passed through earlier. It smelled earthy and clean. I started doing cart wheels through it.

With one final flip, I stopped my tumbling and lay looking back at the house.

There was movement in a third-floor dormer window. Must be Grauntie setting up our bedroom. I shielded my eyes against the sun and waved, but I couldn't see anyone wave back. The house, taking on the glow of the lowering sun, looked better. I could see what a grand old place it must have been.

Standing up, I threw my arms out and began spinning in crazy circles, my feet twisting in the long grass, before getting tangled up in it and landing on my butt.

Charlie ran toward the edge of a forest, so I scrambled back up and ran after him.

He was staring at an arch made of bent twigs and branches. A path left the grassy lawn and entered the forest under the arch. It wound out of sight among the biggest, thickest trunked trees I'd ever seen.

"Let's explore!" Charlie said. He walked through the arch and into the darkness of the forest.

I felt the urge to go too, but I knew Grauntie would be looking for us soon. "Come back, Charlie. This might be someone else's property. We can check it out tomorrow." But he kept walking, and I soon lost sight of him.

"Charlie! Come on. We need to go back now." The evening bugs were coming out. I swatted at them as I made one final call for Charlie telling him, "Fine, have it your way. I'm going back without you."

And that's what I did. Starting back toward the house, a light in a second-floor window caught my eye. This time I could see Grauntie moving about in the room.

Charlie came bounding up behind me. "Hey, I think

there's a house down on that path. Like a playhouse maybe?"

That sounded interesting I thought before taking off running, calling back to Charlie, "Race you back to the house." He didn't bite though. He knows I always win so he doesn't even try anymore.

It was while I waited for him next to the stone wall that I heard shouts coming from down by the river.

6

FIRST NIGHT HAPPENINGS

"You didn't beat me, because I wasn't racing," Charlie said. But Lillia was staring out across the river and didn't pay attention to him.

He asked, "What's up?"

"Shhh. Listen. I think I heard something," Lillia said.

"Don't tease me. I don't hear anything but crickets and frogs. Let's go in." And he jumped over the wall and ran across the patio. It was dark, and he saw Lillia wasn't following him. She stayed behind by the wall.

Charlie hesitated. "What's the matter Lillia? You're the one who said we had to go in now."

Charlie knew he wouldn't step into the dark kitchen alone. His eyes scanned the big window over the kitchen sink. How could it be that dark in there?

"Boo!"

He screamed. His heart leapt up into his throat. "Don't do that."

"Try not to be such a scaredy cat," Lillia said.

"What were you staring at?"

"I told you. I heard something coming from the river area."

"Like what?" Charlie asked.

"Oh just screams and stuff," Lillia said as she brushed past Charlie and opened the kitchen door.

Lillia's finger's groped along the wall, trying to find a light switch. Charlie stayed close behind her. She carefully navigated around the old wooden table in the middle of the room. Charlie yelped when his toe met the solid, unmoving leg of the table.

Charlie issued a weak, "Grauntie? Walter?"

No answer.

"Lillia, find a light. I don't like this."

Footsteps sounded. Someone was walking on a staircase somewhere deep inside the house.

Frozen, Lillia and Charlie waited, holding their breaths.

The steps faded away.

Lillia whispered, "I don't know where the light switch is. Just stand still until our eyes adjust. I don't want to run into a wall."

"Or into whatever was making those footsteps."

"Probably just old house sounds," Lillia said.

Charlie screamed when a door suddenly swung open, and someone said, "Why are you in the dark?"

Lillia clutched her hand to her chest, her heart racing. "You scared us!"

Grauntie switched on the kitchen overhead light. "Sorry, but I thought you were still out running around. Found our bedrooms. This place is quite something!" She pointed at the swinging door and said, "A beautiful dining room is in there. The staff could just push through and serve dinner."

Now that the lights were on Charlie was happier, and hungry again. "Are there any snacks?"

"I didn't find anything. We'll pick some stuff up in town tomorrow," Grauntie said.

Lillia said, "Someone was walking on stairs Grauntie. Do you think Walter is wandering around in the dark?"

"I hope not," Grauntie said. "Lillia, check this out." She opened a door in the corner to reveal a steep and narrow staircase.

"Cool. A secret staircase," Charlie said.

Lillia stuck her head in through the doorway. "Can I use these stairs? I could meet you on the second floor."

"Sure, why not? Come on Charlie. We'll take the grand staircase in the front hall."

Grauntie led Charlie out to the front hall where the

large chandelier was lit, illuminating the stairs. It rose up to a landing with a stained glass window. The colorful glass pieces should have glistened in the light, but after years of accumulating dust, they offered only a flat reflection.

As Charlie and Nora turned and climbed the rest of the way to the second floor, they passed the chandelier at eye level. Charlie leaned over the railing and looked down to the hall floor far below. "Wow. This place is huge."

He hoped Mom remembered to pack his nightlight.

7

LILLIA

The wooden steps were lit by one bare bulb hanging above. No fancy dancy crystal chandelier here I thought. This must be the servant's back stairs. I walked a short flight of stairs to a landing. Then turned to continue up to the next landing where I found a closed door.

With my ear pressed against the door, I could hear faint voices. Grauntie and Charlie are talking somewhere on the other side. Perfect chance to jump out and scare them. I twisted the knob slowly and quietly.

After a few tries of jiggling and tugging at the knob, I realized the door was locked. Bummer. I knocked on the door. But no one came to rescue me.

Knocked again, louder. "Grauntie, can you open the door from your side. I'm locked out here."

They didn't hear me. Their voices were fading away.

Now I beat on the door.

Suddenly the staircase light switched off. I was left in the dark.

I fumbled for the switch and turned the light back on.

Then, just as quickly, it was switched off from below.

What?

Switched it on again.

Off it went.

On.

Off.

I pounded on the door again.

A voice called up. "Judith is that you? Is someone up there?"

Should I answer? Guess I had no choice. "It's me Lillia Pameroy. I used the back stairs, but the door up here is locked."

The light switched on below and the sounds of thump, step, step...thump, step, step...worked their way up. Soon Mr. Meyer's face appeared at the first landing. "My goodness, I had no idea what was going on. I saw the stairway light on."

"I'm sorry if I woke you, Mr. Meyer. Grauntie said it would be okay if I used these stairs."

"Grauntie?"

He looked puzzled, so I said, "My Grauntie Nora."

"Ah yes, my surprise guests," he said, a grin spilling across his face. "Hang on a minute little lady."

He walked back down with his cane for support. Sounds of a drawer opening, things pushed around, and then a grunt of satisfaction before the thump, step, step tune again. This time with an accompanying metallic jangle.

"Here you go," he said, handing me an old metal ring with all sorts of different keys hanging on it. "One of these will fit I'm sure. Start with the biggest one. I think it fits most of the locks in Edgewater. This was the key ring Judith always kept with her." He paused, leaning on the stair railing. "When I was young my brother Robert, sister Amelia, and I would sneak down these at night." He chuckled as he continued, "We called them the milk and cookie stairs."

"That's a sweet story. I'm sorry if I disturbed you."

"Nonsense, it's nice to have some sounds here that are coming from living people," he said with a wink as he turned and started back down. "Oh and turn out the light once you're in the hall up there."

"You got it, Mr. Meyer. Goodnight."

"Goodnight young lady."

I put the key in the door's lock and turned it. Hooray! It worked.

The hallway ran off both left and right. Where had

they gone? Three doors stood open with lights on. The rest of the hall was in shadows.

Behind the nearest door, was a beautiful room. Obviously decorated for a girl. The abundance of pink gave that away. A bed, with a canopy holding a soft cloud of fabric, sat against the far wall. I ran my hands over the delicate roses embroidered randomly across the silky white bedspread. Heavy drapes were caught back at the edge of a tall window to reveal a plump, inviting window seat with a rosy pink velvet covering it. Outside the window the full moon had risen, hanging in the night sky. Scattered clouds were lit by the moon's gentle glow.

In the far corner stood a doll house on a dark wood table. Peeking inside, I saw tiny miniature furniture. Even paintings on the walls. And small carpets on the floors. Wonder who the girl was that slept in this bedroom and played with this dollhouse.

I turned quickly back to face the window when a voice said, "I loved playing with that dollhouse." A young girl sat on the window seat. An inviting smile on her lips made me smile back without even wondering who she was.

Her delicate nightgown seemed to float around her. Her knees were drawn up to her chest, and her chin rested lightly on them. She slowly unfolded herself and sat up straight on the edge of the window seat, her feet resting on the floor. "Judith told me you would be coming. She opened my room and freshened it up for you. I'm so glad you arrived tonight Lillia, because there's something I need help with."

Her figure began fading away. "I have to leave now, but meet me in the attic on the top floor tomorrow night."

"Ah I see you've found your room." I spun back to face the door as Charlie and Grauntie walked in.

"I put your suitcase in the closet. This room has its own bath too. Those fresh roses smell amazing. Judith must have brought them in when she got the room ready."

"Do you think this was her room?" Charlie asked, pointing to the oval framed portrait of a young girl. He walked past it, turned and went walked back again. "It feels like her eyes are following me too," he said, returning back and forth one more time. "Just like that old lady downstairs."

"Then stop moving and go to your room. Her eyes won't follow you there," I said as I walked toward the window seat and peeked behind the drapes.

Grauntie winked at Charlie and said, "I think we're being asked to leave."

I ran to hug Grauntie. "This bedroom is perfect for me. Maybe not all the pink, but I just love the room."

"Night Lillia," Grauntie said, shooing Charlie out of the room and closing the door.

After putting my t-shirt and leggings on, I went into the bathroom to brush my teeth. A breeze came through the opened window. The white bathtub had little feet that looked like animal claws. Wall lights with bulbs shaped like candles hung on either side of a mirror. The mirror reflection showed the room and the window seat. Movement! I raced out of the bathroom. But the room was empty.

The girl had told me to meet her tomorrow night in the attic. Tomorrow night it is.!

The bed cover was turned down for me now. Grauntie must have snuck back in and done that. This girl probably had maids that came in every night to turn down her bed.

This is going to feel terrific. Maybe it's one of those feather beds.

It is! I sunk into the fluffy cloud-like softness.

With lights out, the moonlight settled into every corner of the room.

8

MORNING IN WISCONSIN

The morning sun rose over the farm fields of central Wisconsin. The mighty river flowed as it had for thousands of years, cutting a path across the state on its way to join the Mississippi. Crops of corn, soy, and wheat grew in fields covering the rolling hills. Other fields were cloaked in black fabric to shade the tender ginseng plants beneath. This ancient Chinese healing root found these soils perfect for its growth.

Edgewater Estate had been built by a lumber baron from the East Coast. He had chosen this location, atop a hill above the river, for his wife who loved the view of Rib Mountain. Perched here since the late 1800's, the mansion bore mute witness to the devastation of vast tracts of ancient white pine as the lumbermen cut them down to fuel the needs of a growing nation. She watched cut logs float by on the river, making their way to the family-owned Bull Falls Lumber mill.

Edgewater welcomed her family's guests, offering comfort and shelter in her grand rooms. And she mourned with her family, offering solace when sorrows came. Death took many from her over the years, and she had fallen into a deep sleep.

Something was astir today.

Walter appeared first in the kitchen on this sunny morning. He sat at the kitchen table, his hands cradling a cup of coffee. Dreams troubled his sleep last night. Memories that hid from him in the daytime would hauntingly and unexpectedly find him at night.

"Morning Mr. Meyer," a boy said as he came through the arched opening from the hall. "How'd you sleep?"

Walter chuckled to himself. Been many years since anyone had asked him that. The boy pulled out a chair and sat down, leaning his elbows on the table. Who was he and why is he sitting at my table?

Walter's polite manners took over, and he said, "Slept about as good as usual. You?"

"Not bad. Slept in Grauntie's room on a big chair," he said, looking a bit uncomfortable. "Not that I'm afraid of the dark or anything like that, cause I'm eight years old. I just wanted to be sure Grauntie was okay all alone in a strange house."

"I understand," Walter said. "I'm sorry, but who's Grauntie again?"

The boy laughed, "She's my grandaunt Nora. We call her Grauntie."

Seemed like a nice enough young man Walter thought. Was that little Johnny maybe? An older woman came in next. That must be Nora he thought

"Good morning, Mr. Meyer. And look at Charlie up all bright and early," she said.

So that's his name, Charlie. Good thing I didn't call him Johnny, Walter thought. These people were here yesterday. They must have spent the night. I've got to start writing things down. But why bother making so many notes? What did it matter really? Maybe to avoid sounding like a stupid old man. Be careful, or they'll put you away in an old folks home where you can sit in a chair all day and drool.

Nora said, "We'll be leaving for our morning ice cream soon. I heard Briq's in Merrill has great soft serve. Hope you still want to come along."

Ice cream? At this time of the morning? And I said I'd go along? With a kind smile, Walter said, "I think I'll pass. You all go ahead."

"Oh, I'm sorry to hear that. Will Judith be coming today?" Nora asked. "I'd hoped to meet her soon. I'm going to pick up some groceries while we're in town. Is there something I can pickup for you?"

Where was Judith anyway? I thought it was her on the stairs last night. He puzzled a minute before mentally kicking himself. You old fool, she passed away. The memories mixed up in his head again. Mornings were often like this for him. Usually, it didn't matter because no one would be here to witness his slipping. He hoped he could keep hiding it. He wanted to live out his life in this house, his family home.

"Ah I don't think she's coming in," he said. "I believe I'll skip the ice cream, but thank you for asking."

Nora sensed Walter confusion. "Here's my Lillia now. She probably heard me say ice cream."

"Morning Grauntie," Lillia said. "And good morning Mr. Meyer. Do you know who the bedroom with all the pink belonged to? I slept in there last night."

"Bet it is the girl with the bow in her hair. The one in the picture, right?" Charlie said.

"That bedroom might have belonged to my little sister Amelia. I haven't been up in those rooms for years so I can't be sure. But I remember she loves pink. Just the sweetest and kindest sister a boy could ask for. The Princess we called her."

"Can we meet her?" Nora asked.

Walter's shoulder's dropped, and he said, "I haven't seen her in a long time. I'm not sure where she is."

He tried searching inside his head, but he couldn't find a grown up Amelia there. He gave a quick sharp shake of his head and took in the concerned look from the three people sitting at his kitchen table. "Not fun getting old. Silly all the stuff I can't remember. Think I'd remember where my sister is wouldn't you?"

"Well if that's her in the portrait she was beautiful," Nora said.

"Hmm? Uh, I'm not sure, but probably is." Then, with an abrupt change of demeanor, Walter said, "Well, I believe I'll walk down the drive and get the mail." He slowly made his way out of the kitchen.

Nora said, "I was told Mr. Meyer has dementia. He forgets many things. People with that will sometimes remember something from long ago like it was yesterday. And then might forget something that happened yesterday."

Lillia said, "I think that was happening last night when he found me locked on the stairway. He seemed very confused. Thought I was Judith."

Grauntie Nora laughed. "Hey you wake me, and I'd be pretty confused too!"

"So sometimes he is just normal though right?" Charlie asked.

"I hear the memories can come and go. So I guess yes, sometimes he is what you'd call normal. But we need to realize his normal is still something different than we can even imagine. Okay kiddos, enough questions for now. Ice cream awaits!"

9

LILLIA

I liked the little town and I loved the ice cream. My Brownie Briq Mountain...yum! Brownie pieces, hot fudge, hot caramel, pecans, can't do better than that. We sat in the sunshine at a wooden picnic table eating our breakfast.

"So if Mr. Meyer can't remember stuff is he still coming to the memorial at the fishing hole? I mean it won't matter to him right?" I asked. "He wouldn't remember being there or not being there."

"Good question. I certainly won't force the issue. Guess we'll play it by ear, see how he is on Saturday," Grauntie answered.

Charlie, wiping ice cream drips off his chin, said, "I hope he comes. Otherwise who else would be there but us? Isn't a funeral for the family?"

Nora said, "I've reached out to a high school friend of

John's who works in a town near Rib Mountain. And we're going to visit a farm family John told me about. He said that family was probably the reason he made it until eighteen and didn't leave sooner. They were his escape from the life he lived at the mansion," Grauntie said. "In fact, in the packet he gave me, there is an envelope for a woman on the farm named Anna, someone he called his second mother."

Charlie asked, "Why was he trying to escape? He had a nice house to live in."

"I'm not sure. I think it was an unhappy sort of place for him," Grauntie said.

I knew about wanting to escape home. Mom and I didn't always do so well together. And now with a new baby coming it was just easier for her not to have me around so much, making her upset.

After our morning ice cream, Grauntie drove back out to the country. This time, she turned into a dirt driveway before the stone bridge.

The farmhouse had been white at one time, but now the paint was faded and flaking. Large oak and maples grew in the neatly mowed yard. A red barn, also badly in need of paint, stood off to the right.

"Hey look," Charlie said. "There's a hill built up to the second story of the barn. What's that for?"

Grauntie explained how farmers would drive tractors

pulling wagons loaded with hay bales up the hill and into the barn loft to store them for winter cattle feed.

"So what's that round thing next to it?" he asked.

"That's a silo to hold corn," Grauntie said. "Looks like it's not being used anymore though."

We pulled up near the house. A walkway, with moss growing between the stones, led to the shaded front porch. Overgrown shrubs grew alongside it, and a swing hung from the porch roof.

When a smiling face appeared at one of the windows, Grauntie stepped out of the car and waved. The woman waved back before disappearing from the window and reappearing at the side door.

"Can I help you?" she said, wiping her hands on her apron as she held the door open. A toy sized dog with long white hair escaped, his feathery tail wagging as he raced across the yard. "Peanut, come back here. PEANUT! COME!" The dog barked and bounced around us.

"Hi. I'm Nora Pameroy."

"Sorry, she has a wicked bark but no bite."

A young girl about my age stepped out from behind the lady. Her short blonde hair shimmered in the sunlight as she ran out and scooped up the little dog.

"Thanks, Molly. Sorry about that, you were saying?"

Nora said, "Oh no problem. The kids here have a dog at home, so we know how it goes."

I thought of home and my dog Tucker but quickly pushed the thoughts aside. What was the point? I just wanted to enjoy myself here in Wisconsin and not think about home at all. Though I sure missed Tucker.

Nora continued, "I'm here at the request of John Meyer."

"Johnny? Oh my, I haven't heard from him in years! How is he?"

"Are you Anna?" Grauntie asked.

"No, I'm her daughter Bernice. This is my grand-daughter Molly."

Grauntie introduced Charlie and me before saying, "Do you have a minute? I'd like to chat."

"Oh sure. Let's go up on the porch," Bernice said. "My baking has made the house like an oven. Molly, why don't you take Charlie and Lillia and show them the new baby chicks?"

Molly said, "Sure. C'mon. They just hatched a week ago. They're so cute!" And she skipped off to a small wooden building near the barn with Charlie and me racing to catch up.

The noise of cackling chickens hit us before we went in the door. Molly walked right on in, the hens scattering and scrambling away from her feet. From a big upside-

Locked Doors

down metal umbrella hung a bright light. In the wood shavings beneath it balls of yellow fluff rested.

Molly reached inside and scooped one up to hand to Charlie. "Now just hold on real gentle. Their little feet are still soft so they wouldn't scratch you."

With that, she reached in again and handed one to me. I'd never held a life so small and fragile. The tiny body fluttered and wiggled in my grasp.

Molly stood watching us. "You two are great baby chick holders. I swear some of my friends get all nervous, and I have to grab the chick back before they drop the little thing."

I smiled at the tiny creature in my hand and with the tip of my finger stroked its head. "Thanks for letting us do this Molly. It must be fun living on a farm."

"I don't live here, but my parents both work and so I stay here a lot with Grandma and GG Anna. They don't farm this anymore, except for chickens. But I like it well enough I guess. Are you here visiting someone? We don't usually have strangers coming through unless they have relatives around here."

I said, "We're staying with Mr. Meyer at the Edgewater Estate. My grandaunt has his nephew's ashes to spread on a fishing hole nearby."

"Ashes? What do you mean, spread his ashes?" Molly asked.

"He died and they cremation him," Charlie said.

"Cremated," I said. "Pronounce it right Charlie. They burn the body instead of burying it. Sounds strange, but lots of people do it now."

"The Bible has that verse about ashes to ashes so guess it fits this case," Molly answered with a shrug. "But they don't just bury the ashes then?"

Charlie said, "Part of him was buried in Deadwood. The rest is in a locket Grauntie's wearing."

"Eww! Now that's something I sure never heard of," Molly said.

"Anyway, we have to find that fishing hole John talked about. Maybe you know of one near here? On the Silver Creek?"

Molly screwed up her mouth and tapped her purple sneaker on the floor. "I think I might. That's the creek that runs between our farm and the Edgewater Estate. The best fishing spot is the one near the mouth of the creek, close to where it enters the Wisconsin."

"Could you show us where it is?" I asked.

"Sure." She leaned in closer. "On one condition, that you'll show me inside the mansion. I hear it's amazing, but haunted!"

10

ON THE FARM

Nora and Bernice made their way up the porch steps and sat side by side in the swing. Nora could see why John loved this place. Calm and quiet, with natural beauty like the Black Hills.

"I have a feeling you don't have pleasant news to share about Johnny," Bernice said.

"You're right," Nora said. "I didn't want to tell you the sad news in front of your granddaughter. John passed away several months ago. I'm so sorry. He often spoke of what a great friend you were to him. How your family took him under their wing."

Bernice looked off over the farm. "He's gone too young." She brought her gaze back to Nora. "What happened to him?"

"Cancer," Nora said quietly.

Bernice left out a soft sigh, shaking her head slowly

before saying, "Not that beast again. I hate cancer with a passion. Awful thing. Lost my husband to it."

Nora patted her hand. "I'm sorry to hear that."

"Thank you for letting me know about Johnny. He's been gone from Wisconsin for so long. We've always missed him over the years. Looked forward to his rare visits home."

"Bernice, actually Johnny wanted me to talk to your mother, Anna. I have a small package to give her."

"She's probably taking a nap now. Up in years so I kind of hate to wake her. You could leave it with me. If you're around for a while, I know she would love to meet you."

"And I'd love to meet her. I'm sure we'll have time to visit one day. John was cremated and buried in South Dakota at the Mt. Moriah Cemetery, but he asked me to spread the ashes I keep in here." Nora reached for a locket hanging at the end of a gold chain around her neck and showed it to Bernice.

"Beautiful locket," Bernice said. "Where does he want you to do that?"

"At his favorite fishing spot on the Silver Creek. Apparently, it's on the border of your farm and the Edge-water land. Would you be able to help me find it? Our host, Walter Meyer, seems a bit too frail to make the walk."

Before Bernice could answer, the three children came running around to the front of the house.

"Grauntie, I held a baby chick!" Charlie yelled out.

"You did?" Nora said. "Hope you didn't squish it!"

Molly said, "Nope he did just fine. Lillia held one too, but it pooped in her hand."

Lillia laughed and held up her palm. "Molly showed me how to use the hand pump at the well, and I washed it off."

Charlie added, "It was green poop...yech!"

"Can I take them down to the creek, Grandma?" Molly asked. "They're looking for a fishing spot, and I think I know right where it is."

"Well now, I'm not sure," Bernice said.

Nora thought the Lillia and Charlie might enjoy the chance to explore. And it would free her up to go back to the house and straighten things up a bit.

"Please Grandma? We'll be careful and stay together," Molly pleaded.

Bernice asked, "How would you know where a fishing hole is? I don't remember you ever going fishing."

Molly smiled and said, "I am a bit of an explorer Grandma. Besides, I go with Daddy when he fishes. Please?"

"Fine with me," Nora said.

"Okay, I suppose so," Bernice finally said. "Nora,

how about I bring the kids back to Edgewater when they are done exploring. Molly will love the company. Get's to be a long day here with Grandma while mom and dad are working."

"Oh yes!" Molly said. "Lillia said I could see inside the haunted mansion too."

Bernice just laughed and said, "Now child, don't go believing all those tall tales about it. I've heard so many rumors I don't know what to believe. One of those ghost hunting groups even came to check it out once. I never read about what they found though. Foolishness if you ask me."

Grauntie started saying, "Lillia might enjoy the idea of a haunted house, with paranormal ..." She caught the look Lillia shot her and stopped.

"It surely is a likely spot if you want that sort of thing," Bernice said. "One story about the place goes that an Indian princess is buried there and her father, the chief, cursed the land or some such thing."

Molly's hands flew to her mouth, and Charlie's eyes popped wide open.

Lillia leaned in and asked, "Really?"

Bernice gave a dismissive wave of her hand. "It's what I hear. Off you go now, down to the river."

11

LILLIA

I wasn't surprised Molly thought the mansion was haunted. It had that classic horror house look about it. Up a hill. Darkened windows. Probably tons of spider webs in the unused rooms. And of course the spirit sitting in my bedroom last night would fit the whole haunted vibe.

Guess she could be considered a ghost. To me, she was an imagining. Something, that somehow, my mind conjures up. Most times I'm not afraid of them unless the spirit is creepy or threatens me as the Pirate Queen did. That time I had to swallow my fear to save Charlie and his friend.

Grauntie Nora has tried to help me understand my special ability as she calls it. She calls me an imagineer. She knows something about it because my grandfather, her brother, had it too. Her theory is as good as any I guess. She told me about something Einstein said, how energy never goes away, it just changes form. The way she sees it there are pieces of energy left behind by people who have lived in an area, the emotions they felt, and all that. I'm able to take those pieces and put them into a form, like the girl on the window seat. She calls those my imaginings. The ghosts appear to me because they know I'm an imagineer.

Mom hates my imaginings. They make her afraid of me because of what happened when I was only four years old. What does a four-year old understand? Like I would have known that the dolly I imagined in her tummy was really my baby sister Chloe. When Charlie, her twin, was born alive and Chloe wasn't, Mom thought I had something to do with it. I didn't!

Forget about it Lillia. Don't let her bring you down again. You're with a new friend. Enjoy the day ahead. Mom won't change, and I can't keep getting upset about it.

Charlie and I followed Molly across a field and into the forest where trees offered shade. Our path ended at the edge of a small pool. Further out, water moved along, but right in front of us, it was still.

"Here we are, Silver Creek," Molly said spreading her arms out across the pool, like a bird ready to leap into flight. "And I think this is the fishing hole you're looking for."

Molly has a flair for drama, but it does look like a good fishing spot.

Walking along the pool's edge, Charlie said, "Looks like there are great places for fish to hide."

"I know there are. My dad said so. I like to come and sit by the water to daydream," Molly answered. "It's so peaceful here. A magic, secret, hidden away place."

"Look, a path on the other side," Charlie said.

"We never go there. No sir. That's the furthest border of the Edgewater Estate. Dad tells me that I should stay away from it."

"Mr. Meyer said we can explore anywhere we wanted. I'm going to find a way across this creek and walk back to the mansion," Charlie announced.

"Is Mr. Meyer the weird old man that lives there?" Molly said. "You've talked to him?"

"Sure," I said. "Remember we're staying there. I think he's just getting old and forgetful. He seems nice enough."

Molly shook her head. "Not from what I've heard. People say he prowls around at night scaring little kids."

I almost laughed out loud. But Molly looked so serious, and truth be told, he was sort of prowling around last night. "Well, you made me promise to show you inside Edgewater so you can meet him for yourself. And you can see the room I'm staying in and how girlie it is."

"Cool," Molly said breathlessly. "I can just imagine what a grand old place it must have once been. Beautiful ladies and men all dressed up. Dancing under sparkling chandeliers. Fancy dinner parties. Important people coming and going." Molly clasped her hands to her chest, and her eyes turned upward. "Glamorous gowns. Fine china. Nothing like I've ever seen. Wish I had lived when people wore long gowns. I love dressing up, but around the farm, Grandma tells me to keep it simple, and Mom doesn't like the extra laundry."

"So who do you think is haunting the house, Molly? An Indian princess?"

"I don't know," Molly said. "But GG told me that the family had lots of tragedy in their life. That she was glad she wasn't part of that story even if they did have tons of money. She always says she'd rather be happy in a little cabin, then sad in a big mansion. I say why can't you be happy in both? She just shakes her head and laughs."

"Hey, there's a log that fell across the water up here. Bet we can walk across on it," Charlie said.

I shouted after him as he ran toward it, "Be careful Charlie. Can you find your way home?" Good grief, I couldn't let him just run off like that. What if he got lost?

"Molly, I've got to cross that log and go after him. Could you let Grauntie know Charlie and I are going back through the woods? I have to make sure he finds his way."

Darn, sometimes I feel like I'm babysitting Charlie.

"Can I still come over later?" she asked me.

"Sure. Maybe you can stay overnight? I'll ask Grauntie if it's okay and you ask your mom. That would be fun. We could explore the house together." Especially the attic I thought.

"Why do you call her Grauntie? That's a funny name."

"We made it up. She's my dad's aunt, so she's my grandaunt. So grauntie, kind of like grannie?"

"Ah, I get it now. See you later!" And with that Molly was off to the farm and I was off to cross a log over the water to catch up with Charlie.

My brother wouldn't be the only thing I found in the woods.

12

ANNA'S STORY

Anna knew she was lucky to have such a giving daughter like Bernice taking care of her in her final years. Guess that's the circle of life. But for some the circle of life is different. Maybe they never have children. Or lose a child young. Yes, I'm one lucky gal she thought. It's my time to rest and coast on in the rest of the way.

Gus and I farmed this place before Bernice and her husband took over. This had been a thriving dairy farm. Early morning milkings. Long days bringing in the crops. But everything changes and the small dairy farmers have a hard time making it now.

Now most of the fields are rented out to the ginseng growers. Anna had vague memories of her father hunting wild ginseng roots in the woods, drying it in the hot attic space, and Chinese buyers coming from exotic lands far away to buy the shriveled-up roots. Hard to believe this land right around here produces some of the best ginseng in the world.

A soft knock at the door. "Ma, nap time over," Bernice said, peeking in. "Someone stopped by to meet you. She was a friend of Johnny's."

"Sorry I missed her. You and Johnny, couple of cute sun-browned little ones chasing around the farm. I can just picture you taking off to pick wild raspberries for me, tin pails banging against your legs."

"I don't think many of those raspberries made it back," Bernice said with a wink.

"Cause you ate them all on the walk home," Anna chuckled. "Will I be able to meet this lady?"

"Of course. But Ma, I'm so sorry to have to tell you this. Johnny passed away recently."

Anna nodded. "Felt it might be something like that."

"He requested Nora invite us to a memorial service to spread his ashes at the fishing hole on Silver Creek. Nora left this envelope from him. Look, it says *To my second mom, Anna.*"

Anna reached out to take the small manila envelope from Bernice. "That's so sweet of him to think of us. He was a very nice boy."

"Did I tell you that Molly is invited to stay overnight at the Edgewater mansion with Nora's grandniece? I promised them I'd take them around to tour some of our local sites tomorrow," Bernice said as she left the room.

Anna clasped the envelope to her chest, remembering the young boy Johnny. Another gone too soon. She put the envelope in her nightstand drawer to look at later and went to join Bernice in the kitchen.

"Don't really remember ever going to Edgewater Estate. Johnny always came around here to play." Bernice filled her squat glass coffee pot with water. She reached for the coffee can holding the dark grounds. "You used to work there, right? Like when you were just a teenager?"

Anna looked down and studied the plastic floral placemat in front of her for a moment before saying, "That's right."

"Who was living there then?"

"Well, let me think. Augusta, the family matriarch, was still alive when Johnny was young. She ruled the house with an iron hand. Her father and husband had been killed in a fire at the mill years before. She wore black every day. That was the thing to do in those days."

Bernice laughed. "My gosh, some people nowadays don't even wear black to a funeral. Times sure change."

Anna continued, "Her son George was there when I started. He ran the company for a while, but died during the war. His wife Stella lived there of course. I seem to remember they had three children. Lots of room in that mansion for them all."

"So, you would you have known the old man living there now? Nora said his name was Walter. Might he be one of the children?" Bernice asked.

Anna looked out the window at the farm she had lived on for decades, taking in the trees and the sprawling fields, before saying, "Walter was the middle son. I do have a little memory of him. But I believe he moved away right after I left."

Bernice set the sugar and creamer down on the round wooden table. "Want a cup of coffee with me Ma?"

"Sounds good," Anna said.

"Is everything okay?" Bernice asked.

"Of course it is. Let's go sit outside on the porch swing."

13

LILLIA

I heard Charlie crashing along ahead of me and saw the mansion's roof and chimneys through the trees, so I figured he knew where he was going. In fact, the twig arch we saw from the lawn last night was probably at the end of this path.

I noticed what looked like a smaller trail leaving the main one. I took a few steps through knee-deep wild grasses before the first stepping stone, sunk low in the earth, appeared. Sure enough, this was another path. I knew this feeling. My intuition was strong like that. Whatever was ahead wanted to be seen.

Keeping my eyes on the ground, I found one stone after another and walked further into the forest. I didn't see the small cottage until I was right on top of it. This must be the place Charlie mentioned yesterday.

How cute! Its pink exterior was almost hidden behind

overgrown shrubs. Wild roses bushes tangled their way up broken trellises leaning against the walls.

I'll bet this little cottage was built for the bow girl... for Amelia!

I peeked through dirty window panes and beyond the dingy white lace curtains. Chairs stood near a table that held random dishes. Like someone had been playing and just left it, but planned to return. A doll leaned in the corner of a small floral sofa. On a small side table next to it, lay an open book and a vase holding dead flower stalks.

I could just make out a loft, up a simple staircase. This must have been so much fun to have as a little girl.

It was something Molly would like. I tried the door, but it was locked. The path I'd arrived on, continued on its way, winding through an opening in the forest and down to the river. What a perfect spot. From here you could look out across the river, and over the tree tops to the mountain. Hope that's the mountain Bernice is taking us to tomorrow. Maybe I'll be able to see this little house in the woods from the mountaintop.

The voices startled me.

"I can understand why Rose Cottage was Amelia's favorite spot. She loved roses, didn't she? She would sit here for hours, looking down at the river, letting the sun shine on her. She was happiest here I think." A loud sob broke the words into pieces I couldn't understand.

"Pull yourself together Stella."

"Augusta, I cannot comprehend how I will survive this tragedy. First losing George in that faraway war, then Walter gone to another state to study god knows what. And now this."

"We all have burdens to bear."

Another gasping sob echoed through the air. "No mother should go through anything like this. Why didn't they stay off that river? Robert should have known better. And Kate, my god, they just had a child. And my sweet Amelia."

"Their baby is exactly why you need to be strong. You will have to take care of your grandson."

"It's not right that two old ladies, alone like us, raise a baby."

"Nonsense Stella. We all must do right with what we are given."

This sounded like a conversation from the past. "Hello." No one answered. I called again, louder, "Hello."

"Hey!"

I jumped.

"Who are you saying hello to?"

"Charles Pameroy, don't sneak up on me like that!"

14

BAD NEWS

Since Nora had the rest of the day to herself, she decided to spend it exploring this magnificent house. Her first stop was in the front entry. She reached her fingers in the brass catches of double doors and with an easy gliding movement, her arms spreading, she slid the panels open. The heavy wooden doors, which she was sure weighed a great deal, parted effortlessly, moving into the pockets created for them in the wall.

Impressive workmanship Nora thought, remembering all the sliding doors she'd struggled with over the years. They don't make them like this anymore.

The open doors revealed what Nora's mother used to call a parlor. Two side chairs, with delicately carved arms and legs, sat facing a richly upholstered sofa. Between them, on a small table, sat a stunning crystal vase holding dead flowers. Their water evaporated away. Odd.

Wouldn't Judith clean in here at least once a month or so? Nora barely touched the brown petals but they immediately dropped off the stems. These have been here for years she thought.

Nora stepped to the window to push aside the heavy drapes, sneezing when the dust flew out of them. The view of the majestic trees lining the drive was stunning. What a lovely life this family must have had, living on such a beautiful estate and running a successful lumber business.

This house needs some life in it though. Shame to close it up like this. Maybe someday it could be turned into a bed and breakfast or opened for tours like the Swift-Coles house in Bon Secour.

Nora found tasseled ties hanging on ornate brass holdbacks next to the drapes. It took but a minute to gather the drapes up and anchor them open. There now...let there be light!

She jumped when a long jangly ringing started. A phone? Would Walter answer?

It rang again.

Nora stuck her head out into the hall, peering down toward the kitchen.

The loud rings continued.

No answer.

She walked to a room across the hall to find the

phone. It sat on an oversized mahogany desk. The decision to answer it or not was made for her when the answering machine picked up and Nora heard the caller leave a message.

"Hello Mr. Meyer, this is Mr. Bonner, president at First State Bank. As you know, the county put a lien on your property for back taxes many years ago. No one ever came forward to pay them and claim your estate, until now. I can't fight them off any longer. I've warned you repeatedly that matters needed taking care of. You are losing Edgewater Estate unless you can come up with enough money by the weekend. Do you have any funds left? Please call immediately. WLC, the logging company, is going to pay the back taxes and the mortgage we've been holding in your name. They will own Edgewater Estate free and clear. They plan to take down the old-growth white pines that remain and don't care about you or the house. They are ruthless. Call me as soon as you get this. I'm so sorry we've reached this point. Goodbye."

Nora listened, shocked and dismayed. John's uncle is losing his home?

The answering machine light blinked the number *28* repeatedly. Walter hasn't picked twenty-eight messages up. He might not even be aware what is going on. I must talk to him.

But Nora couldn't find him anywhere. She checked

his room, the kitchen, and the back patio, calling his name out across the grounds. As she turned to go back into the house, there was an answering shout.

"Hello there! Lovely day isn't it?"

Nora looked all around but couldn't see anyone. She called out, "Walter? Is that you? Where are you?"

"I'm up in the bell tower."

Nora laughed when she saw Walter waving his cane from the square tall tower. How in heaven's name did he get up there?

"Can I join you?" Nora said.

Walter gave a thumbs up and replied, "I'll take a lovely lady's company any day. Take the kitchen staircase. It comes all the way up here."

Climbing the stairs had her breathing hard, but the view from the tower was worth it.

With a sweep of his hands, Walter said, "Isn't it grand? This was my great-grandmother's favorite place in the whole house. It was built especially for her. She missed the mountains she grew up with in upstate New York, so her husband created this just for her viewing pleasure. I never got to meet them, but I find their story a delightfully romantic tale."

Nora walked the four open sides of the tower. "This place is amazing. How on earth did you walk up all those stairs, Walter?"

"When I have an itch, I scratch it. I haven't been here in years and years. My grandmother Augusta took out the bell and locked up the tower. She considered it too dangerous and tempting for children. Of course, my older brother Robert found a key to unlock it. All three of us would sneak up," Walter said with a wink.

He pointed across the back lawn as Charlie walked through the bent twig arch and started doing cartwheels and somersaults across the lawn. "Anyway here I am, feeling invigorated by having young people around again."

Lillia was right behind him, but turned to shade her eyes and look up when Walter called out, "Hello there."

Charlie jumped up and down, yelling, "Can I come up there with you?"

"Sure, take the stairs from the kitchen and keep climbing," Nora shouted down.

They disappeared into the house and soon their footsteps pounded up the small enclosed staircase.

"Wow, how cool is this?" Lillia said. "I had no idea the staircase kept going all the way to this. Look Grauntie, in the woods, I just found a playhouse there and I think you can see the roof."

"Hey, I found that yesterday. I told you about it," Charlie said.

"You said you thought you saw it. But, for your information I really saw it. I even went up to it and peeked in the windows."

Nora said, "Kids, stop squabbling. Mr. Meyer is so kind to let us explore his house and come up to this bell tower. Let's be on our best behavior."

Walter started talking about the land they were seeing spread before them. He explained how the glacier ice sheets had shaped and formed much of the area. He taught Lillia and Charlie how to follow the river even if they couldn't see the water, explaining how you could tell where it flowed by the vegetation lines.

Walter's talk about geology and nature invigorated him and enthralled Charlie. Nora would wait until later to discuss the message from the banker.

Lillia was explaining the overnight plans with Molly when a car pulled in the drive. "That must be her now. I'll run down and meet her."

15

LILLIA

Molly was as excited as me to explore the third-floor attic, but first I wanted to show her the bedroom I was staying in.

I'm not sure if I've ever seen a real swoon until now. What Molly did by clasping her hands to her chest, closing her eyes, dropping her head, and letting out a long sigh, was as close to one as I could imagine.

"You are so lucky, I would kill to have a room like this," she said.

"Well, it's yours for the night." I set her pink and purple paisley print bag on the window seat.

"And I thank you for that Lillia!"

Molly ran to hug me and twirl me around. "I just cannot believe some girl actually lived in this room. She must have felt like a princess. I can't wait to explore in the attic."

Not mentioning that a ghost waited for us there, was my way of protecting myself. I'd have to know Molly better before I let her in on my special abilities. Learned that lesson long ago. Not everyone reacted the same. And being laughed at by other kids felt bad.

"I think this could be her portrait," I said, pointing to the bow girl's image. "Mr. Meyer thought it might have been his sister's room. Isn't she interesting looking? Such a secretive smile, like Mona Lisa."

"She is beautiful. Look at that cute hair cut and darling bow. Who's Mona?"

"Really Molly?"

"Hey don't laugh at me, I don't know what you mean about a Mona smile," Molly said with an indignant flip of her chin.

And just when I'd been thinking about how bad it felt to be laughed at. "Sorry. The Mona Lisa is a famous painting done by Leonardo da Vinci. The lady's smile is mysterious. Like she's got a little secret."

Molly stepped back and looked at the portrait from a couple of angles. "Now I understand. She does have a look that draws you in and makes you want to know what she's smiling about. And her eyes. It feels like they follow me."

"Her hair cut is a lot like yours."

Molly fluffed the ends of her hair. "Really?" She ran to look in the bathroom, flipping her head side to side.

"Come on. Let's start exploring," I said.

We climbed the big staircase to the third floor. This hallway was much shorter and didn't have fancy wooden floors. Simple boards laid side by side.

The master key on the ring Mr. Meyer gave me seemed to work in the locked doors we found.

The first door I tried was not the attic. Moonlight pouring in through the dusty window revealed a simple bedstead, chest of drawers with a mirror above it, a straight back chair, and a row of hooks on the wall.

"Maybe this was one of the maid's rooms?" Molly asked.

"Looks like it," I said as I closed the door and opened another one. "This room looks the same as that first one."

We saw two more doors. One stood open and from the hall, I saw shelves full of dusty folded fabrics.

"This must be where they stored the sheets and towels and stuff like that. Can you believe it? I have like one set of sheets. Mom does them on laundry day and puts them right back on my bed. These people lived so differently," Molly said, as she ran her fingertips across the piles of linens on the shelves.

"So that door at the end of the hall must be the attic

access," I said. It was locked of course. I stuck the master key in the lock. It worked, opening the door to reveal an empty, windowless room. Sort of a big closet.

"This isn't good," I said, watching Molly's face fall.

"Oh no...is there another way in?" Molly asked. "Maybe there isn't an attic at all."

"I'm certain there is. Amelia told me to..."

"Amelia told you?"

Oops, I let it slip. I quickly said, "Hey, the other staircase! The milk and cookie one. The servant's staircase."

"Another staircase?" Molly asked. "And how did Amelia tell you something? Did you meet her?"

"Molly, there is a second staircase in the house. I used it last night. And earlier today we used it to get up in the tower. It leaves from the kitchen. But I don't see another doorway here in the hall. There should be one."

"Oh, a mysterious secret staircase...of course!" Molly exclaimed. "The best old haunted houses have those. But how do we get to it?" She started leaning her weight against the walls in the hallway. "Maybe a secret panel?"

Whew, I got Molly's mind off Amelia. "Okay, so are you going to keep pushing until a panel slides open?"

Molly stopped her wall pushing. "Aha...I might have it. You said it was for the servants to use right? It came from the kitchen so they could bring morning tea to the family?"

"Something like that."

"So which room would they use on this floor to do their work? Like discreetly tidying the rooms and the baths later in the day? To get fresh sheets?" Molly asked.

16

WALTER'S CONFUSION

Nora tried to catch Walter before he retired for the evening. A sense of urgency seemed in order by the way the bank president sounded on the phone message. But Nora didn't want to frighten him either. And it was the end of the day. Was his confusion worse now? Or not?

She'd finished washing up the dishes from dinner, or supper as they called it here in Wisconsin. Charlie and Walter had been out on the patio chatting.

It looked so pleasant out there. Cleaning out the dead plants and weeds made a noticable difference. Some fresh flowering plants to add back into the pots before we leave would be lovely.

Long soft wisps of clouds caught the setting sun's rays. The light lavender tendrils, melting into soft pinks and oranges, hung on the horizon. Nature was in a relaxed mood tonight, sending the gentlest of breezes to blow away the afternoon humidity.

Charlie was saying goodnight and Nora decided this was the perfect time to speak to Walter.

He greeted her with a smile. "A perfect end to the day," he said as he motioned for her to sit in the chair next to him. "Charles is a fine young man, and so inquisitive."

Nora chuckled, "Is that a kind way of saying he's bothering you?"

"Not at all. I thoroughly enjoy his company. He reminds me of my nephew Johnny in some ways. You say Johnny has passed away?"

"Yes."

"That's a shame when they die before their natural time. Now me, I've outlived my usefulness to anyone. But I keep lingering on." Looking up and giving a sweep of his arm, Walter said, "But there's enough of me and my brain left to recognize beauty when I see it. And right now this place is beautiful. I wonder if it was Judith who cleaned up the patio here. I'd forgotten how nice it could be."

Nora's ears perked up. She knew she had cleaned up the patio, not Judith. Walter bringing up Judith's name again gave her an opening to find out more about her. "I didn't see her around the house today, but then again I was gone this morning," she said. "How often does she come?"

Walter gave a perplexed look. "She lives here. Once in awhile, she'll leave to visit her family for a day or two, but otherwise, she's here."

That didn't make any sense. Judith didn't live here. "I overheard a message someone left on your phone earlier today, and I noticed you had some missed voice messages. Maybe we should listen to them together, and I could write them down for Judith or whoever helps you with banking and such."

"Oh my, that wouldn't be Judith. Her duties are only..." His forehead pinched into tight lines as he strained to recall. "Now wait. Come to think of it I haven't seen Judith in a long time." His face unfolded, his cheeks sagged and eyes drooped sadly.

Trying to handle this delicately, Nora quickly said, "Well, that's no matter, Walter. The messages will still be there tomorrow. It's late, and this old lady needs some shuteye. Can I help you back into the house?"

Walter didn't respond. A tear slowly rolled out one eye, trailed down the curve of his nose and hung, balanced on the upper edge of his lip. It fell when he said, "No thank you. I think I'll sit here just a moment longer."

17

LILLIA

Molly was already in the linen storage room and pointing to a door tucked away behind the shelves. She slowly opened the door to reveal the milk and cookie stairs passing through here on their way up to the tower. Ahead of us, across a short hall, was what I hoped was the attic entrance. Otherwise we were out of options.

I bowed to her and said, "You do the honors."

"Okay," Molly said, stepping forward to open the final door. "Feels like something is waiting for us in there."

I started thinking little did she know it was the ghost of Amelia when Molly jumped and squealed as a mouse scurried out over our feet and down the stairs.

"Eek...you were right about something waiting for us!" I cried.

Through dormer windows, moonlight filtered down on the unfinished floor. Blurred edges of the beams revealed the dark shapes of trunks nearby. When I switched on the light, dark shadows scurried away into the deep angles where the ceiling sloped down to meet the floor.

Molly gasped, her hands fluttered in tiny birdlike claps. "Oh my, this is just what I dreamt. A hidden room in the castle. Full of mystery. With trunks to open. Clothes to dance in."

Molly leaned against a tall two-doored piece of furniture, reaching her arms around trying to hug it. "Do you know what this is called?" Before I could answer, she said, "It's an armoire. A French word for wardrobe. And it is filled with beautiful gowns. Gowns the princess wore to the parties she attended. Where dashing young men appeared, ready to woo her and win her hand in marriage."

"So open it," I said. "Bet it's filled with old winter coats."

Molly took the brass knobs, one in each hand, and pulled the doors open. Her arms flung wide, ready to conduct a dance of dresses.

Dark coats hung side by side. The overpowering smells of moth balls spilled out.

Undaunted, Molly turned to the next armoire and

repeated her grand gesture. With a final flourish, she spun to me and bowed. "Tada!"

This time she was right. The armoire was full of ladies garments.

Molly caressed the fabrics. She scrambled to reach up to take one of them out, but she was too short. I found a small but sturdy wooden crate for her to use so she could reach the hangars.

She almost tipped off her step stool under the weight of the gown she took out. "Just look at this bustle," Molly said, inspecting the back of the gown. "And the detail in the pearl beading is just perfect against the lavender."

I couldn't resist reaching inside the armoire too. Such rich luxurious feeling fabrics. It was when I touched a long black dress that the first person joined us.

She sat in an upholstered, straight back chair nearby. Her arms rested lightly on the padded arms, bony fingers hanging limply. She turned to speak to me. "That one was frequently worn. After my husband Thomas suffered a tragic death in the lumber mill fire, I wore appropriate mourning clothes for the rest of my life." Her gray hair was pulled back harshly from her high forehead. An uncomfortable half smile broke out below her long nose. "Of course I started adding some touches of white after a year. A lady has to keep up a modicum style you understand. Even in this simple rural place. Back in New York I would have had many dark garments constructed to carry me through the social season. But the social demands here were more limited, and I made do with but a few garments."

Molly swung her gown side to side. "I can just picture an elegant young lady dancing gracefully around the room."

Of course, Molly didn't hear the old lady in the chair. She was my imagining.

"Be careful, this floor looks dusty," I said, reaching to take the gown from Molly and lifting the hem clear of the rough wooden floor. And then another spirit appeared, dressed in the very same soft lavender gown I held. The skirt fell in delicate drapes to the floor at her feet. She stood looking at her reflection in a full-length mirror across the room. "I failed to understand the hardships one would have to endure in this new wilderness. My mother-in-law, Augusta, was already in mourning for her husband, when a dear friend introduced me to her handsome son George. I never imagined that leaving my familiar society to marry him would place such restrictions on my social life." She adjusted the flounce on the neckline, arching her neck and turning her head to admire her image in the mirror. "George changed after we married. It was all business then. Always trying to keep Augusta happy. I was glad I had the children to enjoy. They were the loves of my life."

"Lillia, come here and look what I found," Molly said, peering into an opened trunk near the attic window, oblivious to the other women around us.

18

LATE AT NIGHT

I n the 1800's the lumber baron had chosen this place for his family home partly because of the view of the mighty Wisconsin River flowing past. From here he could watch the timber his loggers cut, float by in wood pens on the way from the great north woods to his mill downstream.

The other reason he chose this site for Edgewater Estate was the mountain view. His wife wasn't happy about leaving the East Coast and the Catskill Mountains of her childhood, to journey with him to seek his fortune. From the bell tower in the mansion, she could easily see Rib Mountain, and that made her happy.

The lumber baron and his wife had a daughter named Augusta. She married Thomas Meyer, and they had a son, George. After his father died in a mill fire, George worked hard to rebuild the mill. But when the old-growth forests of white pines were logged off to supply the demands of a growing nation, the business fell on hard times. And then there was his wife Stella and her extravagant habits. But my what a beauty she was. They met out East where his grandparents had come from and she never truly adjusted to life in central Wisconsin. America had been good to his family though, and he felt blessed to have three children.

The man sat at his desk in the bank, pouring over his records regarding the Meyer property. He didn't often burn the midnight oil, but this was an unusual situation. He could no longer stall Mr. Bonner. The time had come. Mail had gone unanswered, phone calls not returned.

The bank president was on his case. Telling him that we can't keep turning a blind eye just because he's an old man. Earlier today he had said, "The facts are that we have a developer very interested in the property for the timber rights. He's willing to pay top dollar too, plus cover all the back taxes and monies owed us. We'll never get what's owed on the property any other way. Tony, I must insist you speak to Mr. Meyer. Try to talk some sense to him. Or we will foreclose, and that means he will be left out on the street."

The president had ended by slamming his fist into the desk and saying, "If you don't force the issue then I will."

* * *

Anna had just gotten herself in under the bed covers when she remembered the packet she'd received from Johnny. She carefully peeled back the sealing strip and pulled out the contents.

Hundred dollar bills? Goodness, what was this about?

She found a handwritten letter inside and read,

Dear Anna,

I think I may call you Anna now if that's all right with you. After all, I'm not little Johnny anymore. As I write this, I am dying. Don't be sad when you hear about my passing. I had a wonderful life. And in great part, you made it so.

My childhood was immeasurably enriched by having you and your family a part of it. The days spent on your farm meant the world to me. From helping with milking chores, to fishing on the Silver Creek, to breaking bread with you at your big kitchen table, you welcomed me. You can't know how much that meant to me.

I remember how much your heritage means to you. I've made the arrangements to have your family name engraved on stones to be installed at the Pomeranian Memorial. These enclosed monies are to be used to pay for the installation and continued maintenance when the details are worked out.

By witnessing your strong faith, you instilled in me a belief in a life after death we can look forward to with joy.

So on that note, I'll say goodbye and see you on the other side!

Love, Johnny

19

LILLIA

The bow Molly held out to me almost glowed in the low light. I took it from her as gently as I'd taken the baby chick. I raised it to my cheek to feel the softness. A floral scent lifted out of the folds.

Amelia came walking out of the shadows. Her hair cut short with a bow anchored atop, just like in the bedroom portrait. She said, "I am glad you made it. I spent hours playing in this attic. Just me and my imagination."

"She's here isn't she?"

Without taking my eyes off the bow girl, I nod yes to Molly.

The other two ladies faded away, detaching themselves from this moment. The bow girl stayed, strolling over to the dormer window and resting her elbows on the sill. My eyes followed her.

"You see her don't you?" Molly whispered.

How much could I trust Molly to know about me and what happens in my imaginings? She's very into the magical princess thing. Sometimes my imaginings are gritty and not pretty. Should I trust that Molly has the kind of mind that will accept a girl from decades ago, appearing in a long closed up attic?

I said, "Yes I see her."

She didn't bat an eye before saying, "How can I see her too?"

Holding the bow out to her, I said, "Touching this might help. She wore it. Don't be afraid."

"I'm not afraid Lillia. I'm excited. But first, tell me. Is she nice? I think she must be so very nice. And beautiful too?"

My nod assured her, and she hesitantly reached to touch the bow. "I don't see her. Please help me see to her."

Thoughts of other shared imaginings raced through my head. How had it happened? Miss Margaret and I had seen her long gone family. Pete had seen the pirate Queen with me. What helped those people to share in my imagining?

"Molly, I'm not sure if I can." I put the bow back in the chest, resting it on a pale pink dress and took Molly's hand in mine. The biggest grin stretched across Molly's face. Her free hand gave a tentative wave. Amelia, the bow girl, smiled and returned the wave.

"You have brought a friend. My name is Amelia."

"My name is Molly."

"Nice to meet you Molly. That lavender dress you saw was my mother Stella's ball gown. The last time she wore it was the night of the going away party for my father. It was quite an event. I got to stay up late to watch the dancing Everyone was so proud of him. What a celebration. Orchestra playing, champagne flowing. Mother was the belle of the ball. He left for the war and that was the last time I saw my father. He died in that war."

Molly's mouth hung open, and her hand clutched mine. "I'm so sorry to hear that. It must be hard to lose your parent."

"Yes, it was. But now, please on to other subjects," Amelia said.

Molly asked her, "Is Mr. Meyer your brother?"

Amelia covered a giggle escaping her lips. "Oh my, so formal. Yes, Walter is my big brother. And just the best brother a girl could have. It is about him that I reached out to you Lillia. You can help me make something right."

Molly elbowed me when she leaned over and asked, "Why you Lillia?"

Amelia answered, "Because Lillia has some unique

abilities Molly. Follow me up to the tower, and I will show you a few things." With that, her shadowy, soft image moved out through the wall.

Of course, Molly and I had to go through the door. When we saw her figure ascending the staircase rising up the tower room, we hurried after her.

Soon the three of us stood looking out on the moonlit land below us. It was breathtaking. We listened to Amelia's stories of her family. She pointed up river where logs had floated down to her family's lumber mill, explaining that was where the fire happened that killed her grandfather. She spoke of her father building her a special playhouse in the woods, her Rose Cottage, before he left for the war. And then of finding her mother up here in the tower weeping uncontrollably when the news of his death in that faraway war came.

"And right beyond my Rose Cottage, not far out in the river, is where a current caught the small rowboat my brother Robert, his wife and I were in. The spring runoff was strong that year. We lost control of our boat and drowned," Amelia said matter of factly. "I was only twelve years old."

Molly and I looked at each other, shocked at the casual way she tossed that piece of information out.

"This place has seen too many tragedies," Amelia said.

She turned toward us with a smile and said, "But now you are here. And can bring happiness back."

"What can we do?" Molly asked excitedly.

Amelia pointed to initials carved inside a heart on one of the towers wooden columns. "These initials, *WM* and *BK*, belong to my brother and the girl he loved. Sometimes the two of them would visit me at the cottage. She used to work here. She was so sweet and kind. Then suddenly she was gone, and my brother was sent far away to another state. I believe my grandmother Augusta had something to do with it. Mother was very upset, but there was no arguing. If she is still alive, I want you to find her. Her name was Belle."

"I'll help," Molly piped up. "We must find her so old Mr. Meyer and the mansion can be happy again."

Amelia's figure was lifting off the floor. "I have to leave you now. I've stayed too long."

She floated out toward the river and we soon lost sight of her.

Molly clapped her hands excitedly and said, "Look Lillia. Now the river is glistening and sparkling. It's just magical."

20

WAKING FROM DREAMS

s Lillia and Molly watched the ghostly figure of Amelia float away into the night air, Nora, Charlie, and Walter slept. Tucked in their beds, they didn't realize that spirits at Edgewater were astir.

Nora dreamt of John. They rode his old green Jeep through the Black Hills and watched the sunset over the mountains.

Charlie dreamt of ancient oceans stranding him on strange lands. He was fearless, running with new beasts as they evolved when the oceans receded. He wore animal furs and survived the glacial ice sheets. His strength fueled by the cold power at his feet.

Walter dreamt of Belle, his lost love. They were old and sat together on the patio sipping lemonade and watching the gardener tidy the patio plantings. They chatted about plans for the afternoon. A picnic perhaps? Or a walk along the river?

With the morning sun, Nora woke and smiled because she could feel John's presence was still here.

Charlie woke, remembering that today he was going to see Rib Mountain. He jumped out of bed ready to start his day.

Walter woke to a yearning sadness, knowing Belle only visited him in his dreams now. He ached to hold her again. He remembered his grandmother Augusta forcing him to leave Edgewater to go to her friend's forestry school in North Carolina. It would be good for him to learn about reforestation she said. But why then? Right when he was falling in love? Why? The memories swirled, confusing him. He'd written to Belle many times after his hasty departure. She didn't write back to him. All their love seemed to go away. Where does love go?

From all the time he'd spent on this earth, he could only remember pieces of things now. Guess it's that way with most old people. The pieces don't usually make sense anymore. They've lost their order. Time and space and happenings mixed up like the tumbling chips in one of those bingo baskets. Which chip would he pull out of the jumble today? What was the point about worrying about it though?

Walter was sitting at the kitchen table sipping his

coffee as Charlie bounded into the room and said, "Good morning Mr. Meyer. I dreamt about the stuff you were telling me. About the ancient oceans and ice sheets."

"Well now isn't that interesting? I am glad you enjoyed my stories," Walter said. "I dreamt too."

Charlie said, "Do you remember your dreams? I don't always, but I try to. I dream a lot. Like three times a week. Maybe even every night but I'm not sure. Sometimes I think I dream, but I just can't remember what."

Walter let out a hearty laugh. "Sounds like my waking life nowadays. Awake and asleep. I lose my recall of entire days, but then will have a memory of a great sandwich Judith made for me when I was a boy your age Charles."

"Is it scary? The not remembering?" Charlie asked.

"At first it puzzled me a great deal. Found myself getting angry with people because I didn't like their reactions. But then I got to thinking. Why waste my energy? The memories are in my brain somewhere. I do take the precaution of carrying a note."

He reached into his back pants pocket and pulled out a worn leather wallet. A memory pushed quickly past before he had time to see it. He turned the wallet over and over his hand. Where had he gotten this from?

Charlie cleared his throat. "Mr. Meyer, you were going to show me something?"

"I was?" Walter said. The wallet fell open in his hand. "Ah yes, this."

He pulled a note from the wallet and handed it to Charlie. "I keep this with me in case I get turned around somewhere and I'm not sure which way to go. My name, address and things normal people remember are written on it."

"Were you ever lost Mr. Meyer?"

"Haha...not that I can remember, but then you know, I can't remember."

"Gosh, that's gotta be awful."

At that moment, Nora came in saying, "What's awful Charlie? Hope you all slept well. I sure did."

21

LILLIA

Molly and I came into the kitchen as Charlie was showing a note to Grauntie.

"Good morning girls. Did you sleep well?" Grauntie asked us.

Molly said, "Well we were up pretty late. Did a little exploring."

"What were you exploring?" Charlie asked.

Molly gave an exaggerated shrug and funny smile as she said, "Oh nothing."

She didn't know that would only make Charlie more interested. I nipped it in the bud by saying, "None of your business little brother."

Molly and I had talked when we woke up and decided it was best not to tell anyone about our mission to find Mr. Meyer's old girlfriend. It sounded pretty crazy even to us. But the adventure seemed to make Molly happy and she didn't laugh at me or think I was crazy. Plus, she liked all that girly romantic stuff. We'd made plans to return to the attic later today after our sightseeing tour with her grandma Bernice.

Charlie answered, "Have it your way. I don't care. Mr. Meyer and I have our own stuff to explore. Right?"

The door knocker tapping interrupted us.

"Grandma's here! Let's go," Molly said.

Mr. Meyer waved goodbye from the front door as we drove off. He must be lonely living in that great big house by himself. But if Molly and I are successful, we might find him some company. Don't know the odds of Belle still being alive, but we have to try.

"Hey Peanut," Molly said, patting the little dog's head. "Glad to be out for a ride?"

Bernice said, "There's a particular reason I brought her along. She's a Pomeranian. Her breed originated in the area of Germany my family immigrated from, Pomerania. The first place we're going is the marker honoring them. The people, not the dog breed. I want to take a photo of Peanut there and show it to Ma. She'll get a kick out of that."

Molly groaned. "Grandma, I don't think Lillia and Charlie care about some old marker."

"There's another reason I want to stop there. Something I want Nora to see," Bernice said. "And I thought she might enjoy seeing our family cemetery as well."

Grauntie said, "I'd love to see it Bernice. Family is important and how lucky you are to be able to visit their graves. Not everyone has that."

"You're right about that Nora. I can't imagine how hard it was long ago when families left everything they knew to travel to this place and set up a whole new life, knowing they'd never see their families back home again."

We pulled into a graveled parking lot next to a red brick church with wide concrete steps leading to tall double doors. A tall steeple rising high above the roofline, held a large bell.

"This way first," Bernice said as we all got out of the car.

She walked across the dirt road to a memorial stone. "Isn't it beautiful? This area is Pomerania where our families came from," she said, running her hand over the map of northern Germany etched into the monument. "And see these paver stones with the names carved in? All these people were immigrants who settled in this area. They cleared the land, farmed, and raised families."

"Where's our name Grandma?" Molly asked.

"We haven't been able to afford a stone. But I got some great news today. Nora, thanks to your friend John, our families will have pavers with our ancestor's names on them laid here! The packet you brought for Anna contains the funds to do so."

Grauntie's hands flew to her mouth and I caught the glimmer of a tear. "That's so like him. He always thought of others."

"It was the perfect gift," Bernice said. "And he wrote her a wonderful letter. She couldn't wait to show it to me this morning."

Molly held Peanut for a photograph by the monument before everyone walked back across the road to the cemetery.

22

THE GRAVESTONES

The small rural cemetery carpeted the grounds behind the church. Another silent testament to the hundreds of immigrants who arrived in central Wisconsin to make a better life for their families. Headstones echoed the names found at the monument. The orderly lawn was mown and the edges of the headstones neatly trimmed. Small white limestone tablets in the children's section, gave way to tall obelisks with the names of those buried under them taken off by years of wind and rain. Headstone styles changed, and in the newer section, red granite markers, black marble, and gray stone took over. It mattered not the marker, the pastor would say at the burials, this was but a step in a long journey.

"Here is my husband's headstone," Bernice said.

"Grandma, your name is on there too!" Molly said. "That's creepy. I don't want to see that!"

Bernice laughed. "The way I look at it, it's nice knowing I have a resting spot waiting for these old bones. And right over here is Ma and Pa's headstone. Annabelle and Gustave, side by side for eternity."

Charlie wandered off to the furthest corner where a young tree shadowed the ground. A wooden rail fence marked the edge of the cemetery and buffered it from the busy, bustling farmlands. Far out as the eye could see rolled fields, whether ginseng or corn, grazing land or fallow land. In the far distance, he saw the mountain.

Charlie was glad to hear Bernice say, "Maybe we should be going, I have a couple of other stops before we get to the historical society. I need to pick up Ma's quilt from the exhibit and I know they close early today."

"First the mountain, right?" Charlie asked.

"One stop before Rib Mountain. I want to drive you by a spot called the 45x90. Since you like geography Charlie, I think you'll find it interesting. It's the only geographical marker of its kind in the whole wide world," Bernice said.

As the group drove through the countryside, Bernice questioned Charlie. "What is the belt that wraps the earth's tummy?"

Charlie quickly replied, "The equator."

"Right. What is the line going around the up and down way, through the north and south poles?"

Charlie was straining to think of the name for it. "I know it goes through Greenwich, England right?"

Bernice nodded, rolling down her window. The breeze blew everyone's hair around, but no one cared.

"Can't think of the name," Charlie said, leaning eagerly forward.

"It's called the prime meridian. That's a hard one. But now, if we sliced our globe through at the equator and through at the prime meridian, how many pieces of the earth would we have?" Bernice said, easily navigating a curving country road.

"Four!" Charlie shouted. "Four pieces. But what does that have to do with where we're going?"

"Well, Charlie, you'll soon see." Bernice slowed the car and turned it into a nondescript drive. "That sign right ahead of us represents the middle of one of those four pieces of earth. Go ahead, get out and read it."

"Wow...I can't believe this is right here!" Charlie got out to read the sign. He turned and announced, "We are standing at the center of the northern half of the western hemisphere."

"What's the big deal?" Molly said.

"You'd have to know Charlie," Lillia said with a shrug.

"I'm going to visit the other three someday. Yes I am! Can you take a photo of me here, Grauntie? And then I'll get a photograph of me by the other three markers."

Grauntie laughed and snapped his picture. "Pretty ambitious plan young man."

Bernice added, "Do you remember what I said about this being the only marker? The other three points are unmarked. One is in a remote area of China, and the other two are in the middle of oceans."

"I remember hearing about that one point being where a plane went down, and searchers never found it," Grauntie said.

"Well that may be," Bernice added, "but I don't think we've lost any farmers around this one, so I think you're all safe here. When we get to town, the visitor center has a commemorative coin you can collect if you want Charlie. Proof you visited this point."

23

LILLIA

I may not like closed in spaces, but give me a mountaintop any day. The wind was strong up here on the observation tower. The climb up the tower was worth it. What a view!

I had patiently listened as Charlie read a sign about how the rock up here is quartzite and almost as hard as diamonds. He was enthralled, but I ducked out as he started reading more information on another sign.

Now here I stood taking it all in. Below me Grauntie took photos of Molly and Charlie climbing around on the huge rocks. They looked like ants from my high perch. Bernice was sitting on one of the benches giving Peanut a little water.

The Wisconsin River flowed out around the mountain, but I couldn't find the little house I saw yesterday. Scattered fluffy white clouds cast shadows on the landscape spreading out and away from the mountain. Glimmers among the green fields were evidence of ponds and small rivers as they bent and twisted through the area.

The chairlifts for snow skiers in winter stretched down to the ski lodge at the mountain's base.

Far in the distance was a huge lake. It seemed to be getting bigger. Further away white snowy drifts appeared. Must be a cloud bank. I squinted. That was something different. If I didn't know better, I'd think it was snow.

Disoriented, I shook my head to clear my vision. The uneasy sensation of the tower swaying in the wind unnerved me. I clung to the railing thinking I should get down. I wasn't feeling well.

Then a cold icy wind blasted me. Turning my back to it, I turtled my head between my shoulders. This was crazy. What is going on? The wind was so strong that I was afraid it would take the wooden tower down.

I looked for the stairway, figuring I could crawl on my hands and knees to it and get out of here. The blowing wind stopped as suddenly as it had started. I stood upright again and saw a dense glassy wall in front of me, pushing against the tower with creaks and groans. No wait, that wasn't glass. It was ice!

A blinding reflection in the ice bounced out at me. Then I felt warmth on my back. The ice retreated, pulling away from the rising sun's rays.

Screeching bird cries echoed across the vast lands. Strange furry beasts were feeding on the tall lush grasses. Everything was changing so fast.

Smoke from campfires surrounded by teepees gave way to smoke rising from chimneys of log cabins.

Logs floating on the river. Houses sitting next to dirt streets. A train belching smoke in the distance.

"Hey, whatcha doing? You're hanging onto that railing with a death grip." Charlie stood next to me. "Molly, she's up here," he yelled over the side.

Molly tilted her head to look up at me and wave.

"We've been looking for you. They want to leave," Charlie said.

"Ah yeah, okay."

"Pretty cool up here," Charlie said. "Neat how this one high mountain stayed here all this time."

"You have no idea," I said under my breath, glad the imagining was over. Getting blown off the tower, or squished by a glacier hadn't been in my plans for the day.

24

A CRAZY QUILT

The Marathon County Historical Society was ending the popular Quilts in History exhibit. Many visitors had poured over the stories of the local women who had handcrafted the quilts in the display.

Bernice was chatting with the front desk lady when Nora decided she'd slip over to the bank to try and find Mr. Bonner, the bank president who'd left the message yesterday. She excused herself and told Bernice she'd be back in a few minutes.

The front desk lady said, "Your mother's beautiful crazy quilt was a hit. People just loved it. What a fantastic mix of fabrics. Unusual in that time, for a farm family to have such a luxurious assortment of materials."

"Ma worked at the Meyer's for years and collected leftover pieces of fabric. She used some of those in the quilt," Bernice said.

"I heard a bit of gossip around town that old man Meyer is losing the estate. That WLC wants to get their hands on the location. Log off those last beautiful old growth trees for a quick buck."

Bernice said, "Oh no, I hadn't heard that. We live just across Silver Creek. I'd hate to see that forest go."

Molly ran to find Lillia, excited with the news. "Guess what I just heard? GG used to work at Edgewater Estate! Can you believe it? We'll have to ask her if she knew Walter. Maybe she even knew who his girlfriend was."

"Really?" Lillia said.

"And Grandma was telling the lady that some of the fabrics in GG's crazy quilt came from the Meyer's dresses and stuff. How cool is that?"

"What's a crazy quilt?"

"You know how quilts are usually patterns of color and fabrics pieced together? Crazy quilts are all just a piece of this and a piece of that stitched together. All different shapes and sizes of material," Molly said. "We can ask GG about it tomorrow."

"And I think we'll find some more clues in the attic tonight," Lillia said.

Molly tapped her pointer finger on her lips. "Hmm, I've got a funny feeling GG might have known the girl.

Just a little flutter inside me. Do you have those sometimes?"

Lillia just shook her head and laughed. "I sure do."

"Hey let's ask the front desk lady if she knows anyone with the name Belle. She seems like she knows quite a bit about people in the area."

Molly went back to the front of the exhibit and asked, "Excuse me, but do you know anyone in the area named Belle? She'd be really really old."

The lady laughed and patted her gray pouf of a hairdo. "Old like me?"

Molly smiled, knowing what she was expected to say, even though she had no idea old the lady was. "Oh no...much much older than you. Why you don't look a day over sixty."

Bernice just shook her head. "Where'd you get that from Molly? She doesn't look a day over fifty!"

"Oh sorry, right, right," Molly said with a wink. "But back to Belle. Know anyone with that name?"

"Isn't there a pet groomer, works out of her house on Second Street name of Belle? You know who I mean Bernice, that one that does the big old sheepdog Connie and Joel have. If you ask me does a poor job though."

"Sounds familiar. And I go to Belle's Beauty Parlor. So my guess is a Belle involved in that. But my hairdresser's name is Jolene," Bernice said. "Why are you asking?"

Lillia suddenly decided Molly had to look at an unusual photograph hanging on the wall.

25

LILLIA

M olly walked away with me. "Why'd you interrupt? I was getting some leads."

"We don't want them to find out about Amelia. They wouldn't understand."

Molly said, "Then how do we find out if one of them is the Belle we're looking for?"

"Phonebook or a Google search. Simple."

Molly nodded. "True. I don't have a cell phone to search on, but Grandma has a phone book."

"I'll look them up on my cell. We can call later this afternoon."

"Sounds like a plan," Molly said. "One of these Belle leads will pan out. Then we just have to figure how to get her together with Mr. Meyer."

By the time Bernice dropped us off at Edgewater Estate, and we ate dinner, the two Belle businesses were closed for the day. I left messages saying that I was looking for an elderly woman named Belle who perhaps worked at the Edgewater Estate as a teenager. Hopefully, I will hear back from them tomorrow. We were leaving Saturday morning, and it was already Wednesday.

Molly's excitement when she first saw the cottage made me laugh. Her *home alone* expression was a hoot. Eyes wide open, hands squeezing her cheeks, and her mouth in an *0*.

"Wow. All I can say is wow. This is beyond anything I could imagine," she said.

The place had changed. This was puzzling. Maybe the day had been dreary when I came here before? Or I was in a rush to catch Charlie?

Molly tilted her head side to side, before saying, "I thought you said it was all sad looking and neglected. This doesn't look so bad."

"You're right. It did look much worse before. Good thing, now at least we won't have as much work to clean it up," I said.

"We'll spiff it up just dandy. And I hope Mr. Meyer will let me play in it once in a while. It would be great to have somewhere to steal away to and daydream."

"I'm going to ask him where the key is. Maybe tomorrow we can come over and check out the inside."

We got back to the mansion as the sun was setting,

Mr. Meyer sat near Charlie on the patio. He told us the key might be hanging by the door of the little house. Why hadn't we thought of that?

"Thanks, Mr. Meyer. Is it okay if we go inside the cottage? We'd like to clean it up."

"Sure. It would be great if someone used it again. Amelia loved her Rose Cottage."

Molly said, "I visit my grandma at the farm across Silver Creek, and I'd be happy to use it. I'll take care of everything your sister had there. I promise."

"Go ahead young lady. Enjoy!" Walter exclaimed and went back to chatting with Charlie.

Finding Belle might be fun. With no one missing in a snowstorm like Tod had been, and no one threatening Charlie's life like the pirate queen in Alabama, I could relax and enjoy this all. No dangerous stakes, just using my imagining ability in a fun way.

However, Molly was taking this very seriously. "Lillia, can we go back to the attic now? Maybe we'll find more clues."

"That's the plan."

It wasn't long before we hit the jackpot. Augusta's household journals! They were in perfect order, neatly tucked in a leather trunk under the dormer window.

"These don't look personal. Household business stuff. Like we bought this. Sold that. Ordered this. Returned that. I was hoping for some fairytale story. If I have to read about one more potato delivery or how many towels were shipped from New York, I think I'll puke," Molly said, her head buried deep in the big leather bound book.

I was intrigued with the day to day family history logged in the pages. Accounting for the fabrics and buttons and beads to make the dresses we'd seen. Notes of shopping trips back East and hats, gloves, garments purchased there. A horse for Amelia to ride. Train tickets from travels. Employee records.

No visitors came to join us tonight though.

It was getting late when Molly yawned and said, "I don't think we're going to find any great love story here. Maybe Amelia will have a diary in the playhouse, and she'll talk about her brother's romance? Let's head to bed. I'm getting tired."

Quickly agreeing, I scooped up a couple of the journals and a small stationary box nearby to read a bit more before going to sleep, turned out the attic lights and closed the door.

26

THE LETTERS

Back at the farm, Anna was finding sleep difficult. After pouring herself milk to calm her stomach, Anna returned to her room. The hallway she walked down was lined with family photographs. Gus and her on their wedding day. The children and grandchildren in their confirmation and wedding photographs. She blew a kiss to each one.

Still restless, Anna decided to take her crazy quilt out. Bernice had convinced her to put it in the Quilts in History exhibit, but she was glad to have it back home with her. She spread it out across her legs.

Anna's fingers slid across the silky velvet surface of the deep hunter green fabric piece in her quilt, remembering the night Stella wore the cape made from this luxurious material. Remember it swirling around her ankles as she stormed out of the mansion. They had been quarreling again. Anna knew to keep out of sight.

That night it had been Stella demanding to take another trip back East where she came from and Augusta telling her no. Anna could understand how much Stella must miss her family. The ache enveloped her while her husband George and his mother Augusta were so wrapped up in running the business.

Anna thought about how hard it had been to watch the family going through those times. She remembered angry words escalating and doors slamming. She would slip into the back staircase to avoid passing the family in the upper hallway.

I can't imagine being days of traveling away from where I grew up. But then, my ancestors traveled halfway around the world to get here. They left family behind in Germany, crossed an ocean, and traveled hundreds of miles inland to set up their farm. How did they do it?

Look how Molly calls her cousin in Indiana, and they have live video of each other on the telephone screen. Nothing like that for those who left Germany in the 1800's.

In the glow of her small lamp, the fabrics took on a life of their own. Memories came flooding back, washing across her. Pieces of ivory silk damask from fabric used to make

Stella a gown for the annual Lumberman's Ball. What a beauty she was. George so handsome next to her. A soft pink wool for Amelia's dress coat. Her white Easter dress lace fabric next to it. What a precious child. What a tragic death. Another sadness to cast shadows over the Edgewater Estate.

Gently folding up the quilt to tuck it away in her mother's cedar chest at the foot of the bed, Anna noticed something she hadn't seen before. There appeared to be a separate panel inside of the chest. A secret spot?

She slipped her finger into a small opening at the edge, and the panel released. Out spilled a bundle of envelopes tied together.

Anna gathered them up and shut the lid of the chest. She placed them on the nightstand next to her recliner. These must have been something her mother left. Might be fun to go through some days. But right now she was tired and ready to head to bed.

27

LILLIA

With Molly fast asleep, I found myself sitting on the pink velvet seat, flipping through more of Augusta's journals and letters. Right now, I wanted to read the more personal correspondence. Get a real peek at life here.

One letter caught my attention because of the gorgeous stationery it was written on. It was from Edith Vanderbilt, welcoming Augusta to send Walter to her home in North Carolina.

My eyes skimmed over the letter... *I understand your grandmotherly concerns for your errant grandson leaving as soon as possible...unfortunately, I will not arrive back at Biltmore until late spring...I'll make arrangements...Mr. Beadle will welcome him and make him comfortable...excellent idea to engage him with learning forestry techniques at our school...families can be quite vexing at times...your dear friend...*

Augusta shipped him off to another state?

A letter from Walter... *Dearest Grandmother...it is not as cold here as Wisconsin in February...think of you all often and miss you...perplexed as to why you sent me away so suddenly...learning many wonderful things about trees and landscapes...hope to return soon to share my knowledge...look forward to being home again...*

Love your adoring grandson, Walter

He didn't know why he was shipped away in such a hurry?

My eyes turned to another letter... *Dearest Grandmother...saddened to hear of the tragic accident that befell our family...impossible to imagine they are all gone, my dear brother Robert, his beautiful wife Kate, and sweet Amelia...hate being so far away...perhaps it would do Mother good to travel south...spring is beautiful in these Appalachian Mountains...Mr. Beadle is excited with the new azaleas blooming...can I come home soon? Love Walter*

How sad, he couldn't be here to comfort his mother.

Then a different tone in a letter from Walter to Augusta...*Grandmother...mother told me...you achieved your desire...I lost Belle...I want to stay at Biltmore*

Pieces of the puzzle were trying to come together in my mind. Molly and I had found employment records of household staff earlier tonight. We read that a girl called Belle did work here. She had been dismissed in late December and Walter was shipped off shortly after.

But all this doesn't get us any closer to finding Belle. Oh well, maybe the beautician or the dog groomer will pan out.

I slowly placed the letters back in the satin lined box. Resting my hands on Augusta's correspondence box, I leaned back against the wall and stared up at the moon outside my window. There was something here, just out of reach.

These are times I wish I had more control over who and when I have imaginings. I would love to see Amelia again and ask her more about what happened.

The stationery box flew off my lap.

Papers spilled out across the floor.

They swirled into a tornado shape before disappearing.

Words sounded around me...

Leave it alone.
Stop meddling.
What is done is done.

I huddled in terror against the heavy window drapes.

28

IN THE STUDY

S*eventy-five years ago...*

The woman stood pounding the knocker on the front door of the mansion.

Judith raced out of the kitchen and skirted around the huge Christmas tree in the front hall. She peeked out the side window before answering the door to face the unusually demanding visitor.

Judith didn't recognize the woman bundled in a thick winter coat but decided it was best to open the door and stop the noise before Augusta came to see what was going on.

She straightened and stood up tall, before opening the door and saying, "Yes, may I help you?" to the angry looking woman.

The woman pushed past her and said, "I must speak to Mrs. Meyer at once."

Appearing at the top of the grand staircase in her long black dress, Augusta said, "I will take care of this Judith. Please close the front door. I am feeling an awful chill coming in."

Judith nodded and closed the door behind the visitor. Her offer to take the woman's coat was rebuked.

Augusta descended the staircase. "Which Mrs. Meyer are you looking for?"

"The one who runs this household."

"That would be me," Augusta said, waving Judith away and leading the woman to the study instead of the parlor.

Augusta searched her mind to remember any reason she would have encountered this person before. She said, "I do not believe we have met, yet you come here demanding an audience with me. Now what is it you want?"

The woman took a deep breath to steady herself. "We have never met. I'm Wilhelmina Kranz. I don't usually behave this way but I've put up with way too much coming from the Meyer family. I must speak my mind."

Looking down her long nose at the woman, Augusta said, "So speak. Why are you here?"

"First I have to get this off my chest. My husband,

taking on winter work while the farm work is slow, was injured at your poorly run winter logging camp. He's doing badly, and we heard nothing from Bull Falls Lumber. No help with the doctor bills."

"I am sorry to hear that, but it is not my problem. If you have an issue with how the logging operation is run, speak to my grandson Robert. He runs the camps. Now if you will excuse me." Starting to rise from her desk chair, Augusta said, "Judith, please escort Mrs. Kranz to the door. Oh, and Merry Christmas Mrs. Kranz."

Judith appeared in the doorway, but Wilhelmina stood her ground, sliding the pocket door closed behind her, cutting Judith off from the conversation.

Augusta was stunned. "How dare you?"

"I'm not finished here yet Mrs. Meyer."

Judith tapped on the door. "Is there anything you require help with Mrs. Meyer?"

"No thank you Judith." Augusta was determined not to let a farmer's wife intimidate her. "I'm sure we will be finished soon."

"I will speak to your son George regarding my husband's injury, but the main reason I've come is to confront you. How dare you dismiss my daughter without reason or cause? Is it to get all of us out of your way?"

"Your daughter? Are you Belle's mother?"

"Yes I am. She is distraught. She says she did nothing wrong. And we certainly need the extra income she brings in with Otto laid up now."

Augusta sniffed, curling her upper lip and holding a long pause before saying, "Your daughter, your Belle, is an immoral little trollop. What has been going on in my home, I cannot allow to continue."

Wilhelmina gasped. The slap of those words hurt. What did she mean? Was Mrs. Meyer that angry about taking the fabric scraps?

"Immoral? She didn't steal that fabric. The seamstress gave it to her...she's just making a crazy quilt."

A snort came from Augusta. "Do you think I care about some scraps of fabric? Your daughter has been shamelessly flirting with my grandson and luring him into her clutches. I dismissed her because she was trying to lead him astray."

Wilhelmina clutched her chest before taking a breath and regaining her composure. "Are you..."

Augusta snapped, "...sure? Were you going to say sure? Yes, I am sure."

That can't be. This was awful. Tunnel vision took over Wilhelmina as she looked at the woman's hateful eyes.

"What I am telling you, Mrs. Kranz is to keep her away from my grandson. Over my dead body will I ever allow the help to cavort in such a manner with a member of my family. My grandson will be leaving for study with a friend's family. Hopefully he will encounter a young lady more suited to his position in life and of the same religion."

Wilhelmina couldn't believe what she was hearing. Her hackles rose as she said, "My daughter is an upright and faithful Christian girl. Perhaps you should turn those accusing eyes on your grandson. If he has involved himself with my innocent daughter, I want her out of this house as well. We don't need anything from the Meyer's."

Now...

Walter couldn't sleep. He slid the richly carved study door open. His eyes took in the mounted deer head with wide spreading antlers covered in spider webs.

Portraits of his great-grandfather, his grandfather Thomas, and his father George hung behind the massive mahogany desk. Bookcases filled with leather-bound editions lined the wall between the two tall windows.

A sharp and vivid memory came to him, taking him back to when Grandmother had called him to this room one cold winter day.

"Yes Grandmother, what is it?"

"Walter, I believe it is time for you to further your education in forestry. You will be leaving for the Biltmore Estate of my dear friend Edith Vanderbilt. The estate is a world-renowned site for the development of practices and techniques in tree and land management."

"But Grandmother, I don't want to leave Edgewater. In fact, I have found a girl I love, and we hope to marry."

"Nonsense, you are too young to marry. What career have you established to support a family? This is the path you will set on and there will be no further discussion. You leave tomorrow." And with that Augusta spun on her heel and strode out, her head held high.

Could he have chosen to stay? Should he have fought harder for Belle? What happened after that? What happened to Belle?

He braced himself, leaning across the desk's surface and let out an unexpected sob as he remembered the last time he saw her. She said she was taking a leave for the holiday season. She seemed nervous and upset.

Walter remembered pleading with her to tell him when she would be back. He told her he loved her and would see her soon. They had a brief kiss, and she hurried out into the winter weather, the harsh wind pulling strands of hair from the always tidy bun she wore. What was wrong?

29

LILLIA

I hardly slept last night. Whatever, or whoever, took those letters from me, frightened me. It reminded me of the pirate queen's anger being thrown around.

I have to think it was Augusta. She was still fighting against Belle and Walter being together. Why? After all this time?

With the letters gone, I decided not to tell Molly about them. We were no closer to finding Belle, and the letters were whisked away, so it seemed pointless.

"Key was right where he said it would be. Can you believe we missed it yesterday?" Molly asked as she unlocked the Rose Cottage door.

Surprisingly the odors that hit us weren't the ones I expected. A perfumed lightness and sweetness filled the room.

"Isn't this just the cutest place," Molly said. "I love it."

She walked toward the vase holding the dead bouquet. "This will not do at all. I'm going to clip a couple of rose stems from the bushes outside to fill this vase. A house needs fresh flowers. Can you run down to the river to get water for them? We'll need it to wipe up floors anyway. I'll pick up the small rugs and shake them outside."

She continued moving through the room, chatting about what needed doing, as I left to go down to get water.

A woman stood on the river bank. When I got close, she said, "Hello. I noticed you and your friend are cleaning up Amelia's cottage."

"Yes we are. Mr. Meyer gave us permission."

"Of course he did. He loved his sister. You must bring him here when you are finished. He will appreciate knowing her place is alive again. Augusta locked it up the day Amelia died. No one has stepped inside since."

"You knew Amelia?" I asked. Finally, I thought, we might have someone who had been around who remembered Belle.

"Yes Lillia. My name is Judith. I was the housekeeper for Edgewater Estate under Augusta Meyer."

"Wait, I didn't say my name!"

"You did not have to. I am here to encourage you in your journey. You must trust your imagining powers."

This was my spirit guide. Like Emily...like the Irish lady...like Wild Heart. "I remember your name. Mr. Meyer thought I was you on the stairs one night."

"Yes, Walter is a bit confused these days," she said with a soft chuckle.

"If you worked here you must know who Belle is. Is she still alive? Does she still live in the area? Would she want to see Mr. Meyer again?"

Judith shook her head side to side. "That is not how it works Lillia. I can only do so much. You are the imagineer. You are the most important connection between the past and the now. Amelia is waiting for you to help her. Do not give up."

"But what more can I do? I just don't know how we'll find Belle."

"You are learning. Each time you use your powers for good, your strength grows. Be patient. And now, let me help you and Molly."

And with that, she grabbed the bucket of water and started back up to the hill.

I caught up with her and said, "Judith, are you the woman who talked to my grandaunt about staying here?"

"Yes. I made arrangements to answer the phone that day."

I was so confused! "But are you a spirit or are you a living person? I mean how..."

She raised her hand to stop me and said, "We guides can dip in and out a bit. You needed to be staying in Edgewater to help Amelia. I was tasked with making that happen. Lord knows Walter never picks up his messages." She winked at me and grinned. "It is a long story. However, while I am here, I would like to help clean Amelia's cottage." And she was off.

Molly's whistling carried out the opened windows past the white lace curtains billowing in the breeze.

Judith whispered to me as we entered, "I can handle this."

She put the bucket of water down and said, "Hello, my name is Judith. I was just taking a walk in the area and was so happy to see this sweet little house opened up. I have often wondered if it would ever feel a forest breeze blowing through it again. I ran into Lillia here and invited myself in to help." And with that, she started plumping the pink velvet pillows on the day bed.

Molly and Judith immediately clicked, chatting about whether the walls needed washing or not.

30

MIND MAPS

With Lillia gone for the day, and Charlie out walking with Walter, Nora continued her sprucing up of the house. After the memorial tomorrow she planned to host a small gathering. She had reached John's high school friend and looked forward to meeting him. Hope he has some fun stories about the young John. Of course, Anna and her family would be there. Even Molly's parents were coming.

With windows opened for fresh air flow and a light dusting throughout the house, the old place was really brightening up. She filled the parlor vase with fresh flowers. She was energized by the experience of meeting people John knew and being in his childhood home.

Nora was relieved to meet the bank president yesterday and convince him to wait a couple of days before proceeding with the foreclosure. He was nice enough, but there wasn't much he could do. Walter was broke, and the estate was heavily in debt.

Sorry John, wish I could have helped save this beautiful mansion Nora thought.

* * *

Charlie and Walter's walk took them out to the stone bridge over Silver Creek where they stopped to enjoy the view. Charlie had been chattering on about the things he'd seen yesterday.

"Now I wish I had something like that marker you saw. I could use some navigation points in my mind to get my bearings. To understand what's what. A solid marked memory to navigate from," Walter said.

Charlie said, "I know what you mean. I can kind of figure out things during the day, but my dreams take me in all sorts of directions without any map at all at night."

"That's what my days feel like, a dream. Don't know which way I'm going or what's around the corner."

"Mr. Meyer, remember when we talked about remembering dreams?"

"Yes young Charles I do remember that!" Walter said with a self-deprecating laugh.

Charlie gave a thumbs up in return.

"And please call me Walter."

Charlie nodded. "And you may call me Charlie. Now about the dreams, can I tell you one I had last night?"

"Go ahead Charlie."

Charlie explained that his dream had been about the mansion being empty. All the furniture was gone. The rugs and drapes were gone. "It was one of those dreams where I was wandering around and around. It was weird. I kept going through rooms, calling out names. Strange names. But anyway, the thing I wanted to tell you was that the envelope Grauntie gave you, the one from her friend, was just lying there on the floor in one of the bedrooms. Nothing else in the whole house, but that envelope."

Walter frowned. "Envelope? What envelope?"

"The one Grauntie's friend sent for you," Charlie answered.

Walter couldn't place it in his mind. He couldn't remember it.

31

LILLIA

Molly and I worked into the afternoon. The Rose Cottage was really shaping up. Judith had left earlier, and Molly never guessed she wasn't just a lady taking a walk through the forest. I was glad about that.

Our big find for the day was Molly discovering Amelia's diary hidden in a basket on a high shelf.

"She loves all the things I do," Molly exclaimed as we poured over pages of descriptions of dresses her mother wore to this or that gala at the mansion. The beautiful ladies who attended. The flower arrangements.

Amelia described wishing for more friends. How her grandmother didn't want her playing with any neighboring children. She described occasionally go to afternoon teas and meeting children from other prominent families.

We read on through a description of her twelve

birthday party when Molly jumped up. "Gosh it must be getting late. I'd better get back to Grandma's. Mom's picking me up for a dentist appointment. She always says I'm a little scattered and she's probably right."

"Okay if I tag along? I'd like to look closer at your GG's crazy quilt. Plus we never did ask her about the time she worked at Edgewater." I grabbed the diary to continue reading later.

"That's right! I forgot about that. Guess you'll have to talk to her without me unless you want to wait until after the memorial tomorrow?" Molly said.

"No, I'll visit with her a bit today and we'll see how it goes."

When we got to the farmhouse, Molly's mom was waiting for her, and they quickly left.

Bernice and Anna were sitting at the kitchen table and invited me to join them for a minute. I asked to see Anna's crazy quilt.

"I'll go get it for her Ma. Nice she wants to check out your work," Bernice said, as she went into the bedroom to retrieve it.

"It sounds like you two had a fun time at your overnights," Anna said. "Did you see any ghosts?" She made a small laughing sound as her shoulders shook. "That Molly. Always with her curiosity."

I wasn't going to tell Anna that we did see a ghost,

but it seemed like a good time to ask about her working at the mansion. "Molly said you worked at the Edgewater Estate when you were young. Do you remember much about it?"

"I wasn't there very long, why do you ask?"

"Molly, romantic that she is, thinks Mr. Meyer needs to find his long-lost first love. And she's on the hunt for someone named Belle."

"Is that why you two wanted to know about my beauty shop and dog groomer?" Bernice said as she came back out carrying the quilt. "Did Mr. Meyer put you two up to it? That's crazy. He's an old coot and that Belle person would be just as old. Probably married and gone. Molly and her goofy ideas about romance. Goodness."

"Did you ever meet anyone named Belle while you were there?" I asked Anna.

An awkward pause followed before Bernice said, "Ma has a story about every one of these quilt fabrics don't you Ma?"

My attention was drawn to the kaleidoscope of color and stitches and textures being spread out across the table.

"Yes, I do," Anna said, running her finger across a small floral print fabric. "This was from my favorite blouse when I was growing up. We didn't have all the clothes you girls do now. Wore this blouse plum out. Wearing it always made me feel so special."

"You still like those bright yellow colors Ma. Just look at that apron you have on."

My phone dinged that a text message had come in. I reached in my pocket to silence it. I spent the next ten minutes listening to Anna tell stories of the different fabrics in the quilt.

"What was this one from?" I asked, reaching across to touch a ruby colored fabric.

"That was from a dress Ms. Stella had made for a Christmas Ball. She was planning to wear it in a formal portrait as well I believe," Anna said. Her voice lowered as she added, "But I was no longer working there and never got to see her in it."

I looked up at Anna, but she quickly averted her eyes and pointed to a red and black check fabric. "You must recognize this one Bernice."

"I sure do. That Pa's favorite shirt right?"

Now I felt my phone vibrate with a call coming in. Might be one of the Belle leads responding. I excused myself and said my goodbyes.

32

MORE LETTERS

"What a sweet girl," Bernice said. "And to get it set up for Molly to play in that little cottage thing the Meyer girl had. It'll give her something to do on these long summer days. You ever go to the cottage while you worked there Ma?"

Anna said, "I think I might have. That was so long ago, so far in the past."

"Such foolishness with those two. All that about finding some long-lost love," Bernice said, shaking her head side to side as she stood to fold the quilt.

Anna pushed herself up from the table. "Is it okay if I just eat a light supper in my room tonight? I'm feeling a bit more tired than usual."

"Might be some stress about going to that memorial service tomorrow. Think you can make it down to the creek?"

Anna said, "All I can do is try."

"I've got an idea," Bernice said. "How about I set you up with some iced lemonade by the stone bridge? You'll be able to see down to where we'll spread the ashes on Silver Creek. I can drive you there so it would mean just a few steps of walking, instead of all the way across the fields."

"That sounds like an excellent idea. I'll do that."

Hearing Walter's name mentioned again today had hit Anna hard. Memories of the day she was fired from the staff at Edgewater Estate swirled at her as soon as she reached her room.

Mother had asked… *What did he do to you?*

I told her…*Nothing mother, nothing. I wish you hadn't gone over there. You've only made it worse.*

We never spoke of it again.

No promised letters from Walter came. Then on a cold February day, the idea that I could leave home came to me. I could take a job as a nanny or a housekeeper in another state. I'd leave all this behind. Travel the world. Maybe even go to North Carolina.

But I didn't.

Pa died on the first warm day of spring. The widow maker, the limb sawed wrong that crashed down on him, had lived up to its name. Mother was a widow now. So I stayed to help work hard the farm.

Shortly after that I met Gus, a good man, we fell in love and married, settling on this farm. We had a wonderful life together and were blessed with healthy children. My dreams of Walter and travel were locked away. Best it stay that way.

"Got a book to read tonight?" Bernice asked as she came in with Anna's supper tray.

"I found a packet of letters in my mother's chest. The one you brought over from the old farmhouse in Edgar. Think I'll go through some of those after I finish this supper."

"All right then. I'm going to watch a Hallmark movie and hit the hay afterward. See you in the morning."

When Anna finished her meal, she decided to unbundle the packet of letters her mother had saved.

The first one was addressed to her, with a return address from North Carolina. Her heart rose up in her throat. With trembling hands, she tried to open the envelope flap. It was sealed shut.

Anna quickly checked the other envelopes. They all were to her and were all unopened!

Every letter in the pile that spilled across the bed was addressed to Miss Annabelle Kranz and came from North Carolina.

The dawning of what this meant shook Anna to her

core. Her mother had kept his letters from her. He did write. Dozens of times.

She pulled one out of the pile and ripped it open, the words blurring through her tears...

Dearest Belle,

How I miss you! Please write. I must hear the words saying you understand that I am trying to get Grandmother to bring me back home...

All my love, Walter

Dearest Belle,

This is so hard. My heart aches for you. I check the mail daily....

All my love, Walter

Dearest Belle,

Please forgive my tardiness in writing this week, but it has been quite busy here. Still no news on when I'll be back. Mother is trying to convince Grandmother to change her mind. I am going crazy with the time we have been apart....

With my love, Walter

Dearest Belle,

Why haven't I heard from you? Spring is coming, and the flowers are beautiful here.

Love, Walter

Dear Annabelle,

The summer in North Carolina is hot and muggy.

Though I still long to be back in Wisconsin, less so now that I learned of your recent marriage....I wish you the best.

Sincerely, Walter

33

LILLIA

I was so disappointed by the text message from the dog groomer. Her business was named after her dog Belle.

The phone call I'd missed came from Jolene, Bernice's hairdresser at the Bella Beauty Parlor. I called her back.

"Thanks so much for returning my call," I said. "Was my voice message confusing?"

Jolene laughed and said, "It was. But I think the jest of it was you want to know where the salon name comes from?"

"Yes." I held my breath, fingers crossed, hoping it was the Belle we needed to find.

"It was named after my great-grandmother."

Hooray, this was sounding good.

Jolene proceeded to tell me stories about her great-grandmother named Belle. How she always loved keeping herself looking pulled together. "Hair, nails you name it. But Lillia, I don't think she's the person you're looking for. She died over sixty years ago. I never got to meet her, but I decided I'd name my business after her."

Bummer. So close. But wait a minute. It could still be Walter's Belle. "Do you know if she ever worked at the Edgewater Estate when she was young?"

Jolene said, "Edgewater Estate? Don't know what that is. But she lived in Iowa her entire life. I just moved here about ten years ago because my husband was transferred by his employer."

"Okay thanks so much for calling back."

I finished my walk, crossing Silver Creek, past the path to the cottage, and out to the lawn of Edgewood.

The sun was setting.

Charlie, Grauntie and Mr. Meyer sat outside as I climbed the slope to the patio.

Grauntie had been busy. There were new flowers planted in the pots and colorful cushions on the furniture.

"This looks great," I said.

"Doesn't it though," Walter said. "Nora did this all while Charlie and I took a lovely walk down the road today. She is one dynamic lady. How does the Rose Cottage look? Did you and your friend get it tidied up?"

"We did Mr. Meyer. Molly is really going to enjoy playing there," I answered.

"As I told young Charles here. Oops, as I told young Charlie here," Walter said. "Please call me Walter."

"Well then Walter, how was your walk with my little brother?"

"Charlie and I had a dandy day. It worked out perfectly because I was wondering how on earth I would make it through the woods and down to the creek for the memorial tomorrow. We stopped at the stone bridge on our walk and Charlie had an excellent idea. Tell them, young man," Walter said.

"The Silver Creek goes under the bridge. I guessed that Walter could sit on the bank and see to where the fishing hole is. And he can!" Charlie finished.

"Nora, if you'll be so kind as to drop me off there before the service?"

"My pleasure Walter," Nora said.

I decided to excuse myself to finish reading the diary in my room. On the way to the stairs, I paused at the portrait of the lady in the dress made from the ruby fabric in Anna's quilt. So Anna never saw the finished holiday gown on Stella. Augusta let Belle go right around that time too. Odd coincidence? Or something more?

As I stepped away, the sense of the eyes following happened yet again. I went back to look more closely at how the artist did that. The angle of the body maybe? Or her position in the chair?

Stella Meyer blinked.

Her right hand resting on the arm of the chair turned palm up and reached toward me.

Soft music started. Violins pulled and held notes of familiar Christmas carols.

Barely visible people milled around me chatting and laughing.

Piney smells mingled with ginger and cinnamon.

I reached to touch her hand as she murmured,

Don't let Augusta stop you.
I did, and I regret it.
Be strong for them.

34

THE STONE BRIDGE

The next morning Grauntie got Walter settled on the grassy slope just below the bridge. "Are you comfortable?" she asked.

"Yes, thank you. I'm glad we found this spot for me to sit."

"Now don't go getting up or trying to move around too much. You might slip and slide into the water."

Walter chuckled. "If that happens I'll be sure to wave to you all as I float on through the fishing hole on my way to the Wisconsin River." He took off his hat and ran his fingers through the waves of his silvery hair. "Good to hear the water and feel the sun on my face. Easy to understand why Johnny wanted part of himself to rest here."

"Me too," Nora said. "Looks like some pretty thick

woods along the banks. Sure you can see okay from here?"

"Go on along now, they'll be looking for you."

Nora scurried back up the incline to the roadway and Walter heard her car drive away. He reached for a pebble and skipped it across the water. Used to be able to skip a stone pretty darn good he thought. He tried again. Better.

A car stopped on the bridge and the doors opened. His first thought was Nora forgot something, but then he heard voices.

"Ma, this is where I thought you'd be able to watch us from."

"This looks lovely. I'm sorry to be a bother to you all."

Walter turned to look up at who was coming. An older woman peeked over the bridge railing. Now who could that be? Someone else watching from here? When she saw him, she gave an awkward wave before turning to speak to someone. "A man is sitting down there. I don't want to bother him."

A young girl stepped in next to her and said, "Oh hello Mr. Meyer. Remember me?" Anna gasped when she heard the name.

Molly continued, "Do you mind if my GG joins you down there?"

"To have company here would be lovely. Are you from the farm family Johnny knew?"

"Yes, Mr. Meyer. I'm Molly. We met when I stayed overnight at your house. And this is my great-grand-mother. It looks like we had the same idea you guys did! Is it okay if she sits with you?"

Bernice thought her mother looked a little faint. "Will you be okay? You look pale. Would you rather skip this and go back to the house?"

Anna looked up at her daughter. What she saying? Then she turned to look back down at the man she hadn't seen in over seventy years. "I'll be fine," she said, but the thought of sitting by him once again made her a bit dizzy.

Molly watched the exchange between GG Anna and Grandma. What was it? Something was in the air. That little flutter was happening.

Walter, shielding his eyes from the sun, called up to Molly. "Of course. I'd welcome a lovely lady's company. And the blanket here will fit two."

35

LILLIA

Everyone was gathering for the memorial at Silver Creek.

"Did you talk to the two Belles?" Molly said as she walked up to me.

"Dead end," I said with a shrug. "But Molly, last night..."

Molly said,"Hold on, can I tell you what just happened? I just had a flutter moment."

"You did?"

"We dropped GG off at the bridge. Mr. Meyer was sitting there already."

"He decided that walking through the woods might be too hard for him," I said.

"When she saw him sitting there, I got the flutter feeling," Molly said. "I thought they would have known each other. After all they are neighbors. But it seemed like he didn't recognize her."

I laughed. "Guess it's not like they leaned on the fence and chatted with each other every day. Their places are acres apart."

I heard Grauntie say, "Girls come along now. We're ready to do the ceremony."

"I'll talk to you when this is over. Something is going on," I whispered.

Molly's instincts were good. I knew I had to talk to her about what I discovered last night in Amelia's diary and what I learned about her great-grandmother.

We gathered around Grauntie as she started to speak.

"I want to thank you for joining me here today to say goodbye to John. He asked me to read this letter," she said. "Please forgive me if I stumble over it, I haven't read it before today."

Nora,

I hope you laugh at the idea that I would do this...write my farewell letter and ask you to read it out loud!

Ah, there, I hear it. Your laughter was always easy on my ears.

Please read this when you spread my ashes in Wisconsin

and thanks for doing this for me. I could always count on you.

In hopes that some of you are here with Nora, I write the following.

Heaven is my dream of what comes next, but it'll be hard to beat the simple joys the world has shared with me, like how I felt as a young boy at this fishing hole. And most importantly, how you all made me feel.

To my buddy Tony Miller. You might not realize this, but you were the best friend I could have asked for. We lost touch later in life, but I thought of you often. As I return here, to where I grew up, I want to thank you.

And warm love and gratitude to my second family. Sharing your life with me, the shy little boy next door, meant I knew the openness and generosity of a big loving family. Anna, you were like a second mother, treating me as one of your own children. Bernice, you were the little sister I never had. The times we spent together, at the river and in your home, stayed with me and brought me smiles for the rest of my life.

Endless thanks to my own family. Though we certainly had our ups and downs, because of you I had a home and a family to call my own. You're all gone now except Uncle Walter. We didn't know each other well but reconnected later in life. You were off learning about trees and nature most of my childhood. That was the biggest inspiration in my choice to make a move to the Black Hills and live in nature's beauty and bounty.

Lastly to my dear Nora...you were my companion and love on my earthly journey and what you brought to my life is immeasurable and never ending.

Goodbye all. See you on the other side where I believe heaven will be sweet and good and beautiful.

John Meyer

The emotion welled up in Grauntie as she kissed her locket before opening it and lifting it over his fishing spot. John's ashes floated in the air then drifted down into the waters.

36

MEMORIES

"Hello," he said, extending his hand. "May I help you to your seat?"

He doesn't remember me. Have I changed that much? Old fool. Of course you changed. You married, farmed, raised children and grew old...what can you expect? She accepted Walter's hand to help seat herself on the blanket.

"Thank you," she said. "My name is Anna." There was no point in telling him she was no longer known as Belle. She slowly pulled her hand out of his. Belle was gone.

He sat down next to her and accepted her offer of a cold drink of lemonade. "Oh my, that hits the spot."

"Nora is such a lovely lady. I'm glad Johnny had her in his life. I didn't know him well, to be honest, but he seemed like a fine man," Walter said.

"He was," Anna replied. "He was a good boy. He spent quite a bit of time at our house over the years. Played with my children."

"I was gone from here most of my life. Left when I was about seventeen."

Anna felt old feelings rise up in her as she asked, "Why did you move away? Where did you go to?"

"Wasn't my choice. I was tricked you might say. Went to the Biltmore Estate in North Carolina."

Anna nodded. "Oh look she just spread his ashes. Time for us all to say goodbye."

Walter turned to peer downstream. "Yes, I suppose it is." He turned back to Anna and said, "He's back home now."

Walter watched Anna brush aside strands of hair the wind had pulled loose from the tidy bun at the nape of her neck. He struggled to hang onto the thin thread of a memory and weave it into what was happening here.

37

LILLIA

I bowed my head and listened as Tony said a simple prayer thanking God for taking John into his welcoming arms.

When I opened my eyes the first thing I saw was sunlight shining down on the stone bridge and Walter and Anna sitting there. They were smiling.

Molly pulled me aside as we started on the path back toward the mansion. "I think there's something between Mr. Meyer and GG. What was it you were going to tell me?"

"I think they might have known each other when she worked at the house. In fact, I found proof." We were interrupted when Molly's parents asked to see the Rose Cottage and everyone turned in at the little stone stepping path toward the cottage.

It was perfect. Wild roses bloomed, climbing up sturdy upright trellises. The windows sparkled in the sunlight. Everyone crowded in as Molly showed them all the things we'd worked on.

"Well goodness you girls did a great job," Bernice said. "This is precious!"

"We had some help from Judith, a lady who happened to find us working here."

"Judith?" Grauntie said. "I keep missing her."

Grauntie knew about my imagining powers. Maybe I could explain about Judith on the drive back to Kansas. She's heard about my other spirit guides and will understand.

"Come around back for the view down to the river," Molly said. She explained how poor Amelia, along with her brother and his wife, drowned during the high spring waters.

"My goodness, how did you find that out?" Bernice asked.

"We found some old stuff in our time in the attic," Molly said as she winked at me.

Nice recovery Molly...thanks for not letting everyone know about our conversation with the ghost of the girl who drowned.

As we were leaving, I saw Amelia and Stella. They

were walking up toward the cottage from the riverbank. It looked like Molly might have company here after all. I gave a tentative wave in their direction, and their words *thank you*, came through my body.

38

WALTER REMEMBERS

"The service is over," Anna said, looking into Walter's eyes.

Walter kept pulling at that memory thread. He knew her, didn't he? He flashed back to a snowy day and a different goodbye.

The eyes that had swept Anna's heart away all those many moons ago, had dimmed with time and old age. What had she been hoping for anyway? She stood up and said, "Bernice is picking me up here after the service. It was nice chatting with you Walter."

Walter stood as well. "You said your name was Anna. I knew a girl named Belle once, but her full name was Annabelle."

"You did?" Anna said. "I knew a girl who used to call herself Belle as well. A very long time ago."

Walter reached to brush his trembling fingers gently

through the loose strands of hair blowing in the summer breeze. "I loved Belle but lost her. The biggest regret of my life. Do you think I might find her again one day?"

Anna's breath caught in her chest. Her eyes moistened as she reached her hand to touch Walter's cheek and say, "I have a strong feeling that you will find her. And she will be happy you did."

39

LILLIA

I helped Grauntie set out cookies and lemonade for the guests on the back patio while Bernice went to pick up Walter and Anna. I waited eagerly for their return. Anna will remember Walter, but with his mind the way it is, I was worried he might not remember her. Fingers crossed that the hopes of Amelia come true.

I pulled Molly aside to tell her what I'd read in the diary last night. "You remember how Amelia described everything in her diary, down to what shoes the ladies wore? I found an entry where she described what Belle wore when she visited the cottage with Walter. Molly, you might not believe this, but in the crazy quilt, your GG had that exact fabric and said it was from her most favorite blouse ever!"

Molly could hardly contain herself. "Are you kidding

me? Is my GG the one we've been looking for? But his girlfriend's name was Belle and GG's name is Anna."

"This is the most amazing thing! Remember when we were at the cemetery and your grandma was showing us the family headstones?"

Molly said, "Sure I remember, but what does that have to do with this love story we're trying to put together."

"You didn't like it that people who weren't dead yet had a headstone with their name on it."

"That is creepy to me. Just wait till a person is dead before you put their name on a grave marker."

"Molly, on your great-grandmother's headstone, her name isn't Anna."

"What? I didn't notice that! So if her name isn't Anna, is it Belle? That would be perfect!"

"No it isn't Belle either," I said in a teasing tone.

Molly crossed her arms and said, "Okay smartie. What is my GG's name?"

I took her by the shoulders, looked straight in the eyes and said, "Annabelle!"

Molly exclaimed, "Oh my gosh. We did it! We did it! We found Belle!"

"What on earth are you shouting about?" Bernice asked as she walked out to the patio with Walter and Anna.

Everyone's eyes were on us. Now what? How could we explain what we were excited about?

"Ah, Molly and I, we, ah, sort of…" I watched Anna and Walter's reaction.

Anna started to speak. "I believe that Molly and Lillia are excited that they found the answer to their mystery."

"Mystery? What mystery?" Charlie said.

Tony said, "Hey I like a good mystery. What is it?"

"They found out who Walter's first love was," Anna said. "I'll explain in a moment. First I'd like to take a seat and enjoy this beautiful patio with the view of the river and the mountain. I'll have some cookies and lemonade, please. It's been way too many years since I've been here."

Walter guided her to one of the newly cushioned patio chairs.

40

ALL IS WELL

The day turned into evening and a group trip out for a Friday night fish fry, which Walter assured Nora was a necessary Wisconsin tradition to experience.

Sitting in the Eagles Club dining hall in Merrill, Walter kept glancing over at Belle, not believing they had found each other again. He felt more clear headed than he had in years.

So many questions were being asked about the long ago relationship that finally Anna raised her hands and said, "Enough for tonight! Let's enjoy this meal together and talk about Johnny. Nora, you're leaving tomorrow, so could you please fill us in on the Johnny you knew and the life he led since he left Wisconsin?"

The conversation shifted to stories about John from everyone gathered around the table. When the bill came,

Walter insisted on paying. He reached into his back pocket and pulled out his old brown wallet.

"That's a unique leather piece Walter," Tony said. "Looks like it has seen many years of use."

Walter nodded as he slowly counted out the bills necessary to pay.

With a gleam in her eyes, Anna said, "I gave that to him before he left for North Carolina. My grandfather worked in leather. He handcrafted it."

Walter said, "Looks like I've got to keep you around to remind me of a lot of things."

Hugs and goodbyes were exchanged in the parking lot.

Nora overheard Tony say he would see Walter in the morning about that matter regarding the house. Nora couldn't help but think that Walter soon wouldn't have a home to worry about. It would be gone.

Tomorrow would come with its bad news. And what would be would be. At least there was a new light in Walter's eyes tonight.

Walter woke Saturday morning. He had written himself some notes about what happened yesterday, fearful of what memories would be gone in the morning. But they weren't gone. He remembered everything.

Of course he had played it over and over in his mind before falling asleep.

The house hadn't looked so beautiful since he'd come back home. Was it his new lease on life? Or Nora's hard work?

Lillia and Nora came in the kitchen and soon the running thumps of Charlie on the stairs announced his arrival.

Nora asked the children to take their breakfast cereal out to the patio as she had to talk with Walter privately for a few minutes. "And when you've finished, you can run upstairs and pack your bags."

This would be so hard. But she had to give Walter a heads up about the bank president coming today to foreclose on his home and that everything would go to a logging company.

Nora hoped that with Walter's clarity of mind he might better be able to handle this confusing information she was about to tell him.

41

LILLIA

I wondered why Grauntie sent us out. "Charlie, do you know what they're talking about?"

"Nope," he said, shoveling cereal into his mouth. "Know what I dreamt last night?"

"Don't talk with your mouth full. And how would I know what you dreamt about?"

"There was..."

"Chew and swallow first. It's disgusting to see your half eaten cereal!"

Charlie quickly swallowed. "There was that packet again. This time though I grabbed it and ran, chasing after some cars and buggies and trucks and bunches of vehicles driving away. Course it was a dream, so I didn't catch them. But I sure tried...running hard."

Him and his dreams I thought. I almost asked him what package he meant, but then the story would go on and on. Besides, I could see Grauntie had left the kitchen table, so maybe we could go pack now.

"Dreamt about it again last night," Charlie told Walter with a grin as he passed him at the table.

"Did you now? Your dreams are right on target young man. Follow me."

Walter led us out to the front hall where a man carrying a briefcase stood next to Grauntie.

"Good morning," Walter said.

"Morning Walter," the man answered. "Do you remember me, Mr. Bonner, president of First State Bank? I'm sorry to be coming with such bad news. I tried to keep this foreclosure away for as long as I could."

Another car sped up the driveway and slid to a stop. Tony got out and hurried up to the front door, carrying a brown envelope.

Mr. Bonner had a shocked look on his face. "What are you doing here? You're supposed to be at the bank."

"Please everyone, come in," Walter said. "Tony is here on bank business. My bank business."

"What's happening," I asked Grauntie, who seemed as confused by Tony's appearance as the bank president was.

Walter turned to Charlie and said, "This young man, Charlie Pameroy, and his dreams, may have saved the day."

Grauntie and I watched in astonishment as Walter and Charlie did a fist bump.

"Now if you'll excuse us we have some business to handle," Walter said. "I'm sure we'll be just a few minutes, and then I'll be out to say goodbye to my wonderful guests." And with that, Mr. Bonner, Tony, and Walter stepped into the study and closed the door behind them.

By the time we had the car loaded for our drive back home, the three men had finished.

It turns out Walter had finally opened that packet from John, thanks to Charlie, and discovered what his nephew had left him. Walter, confused by just what the paperwork meant, had given it to Tony yesterday. "When I heard John's friend was a banker, figured I'd let him take a look at it," Walter told us.

Mr. Bonner said, "And I'm glad you did that Mr. Meyer."

"Thanks to Nora for giving me the heads up about you coming this morning. I called John to race over here and help me handle whatever was going to happen. I was astounded by the value he had calculated the stock certificates John left to me were worth. Luckily it will cover the taxes and mortgage with some to spare."

Tony added, "And I'll be sure to keep Walter's

finances straightened out so he can relax and enjoy time with his new lady."

Grauntie said, "That's great news, Walter!"

"Well now, lookie who's here," Walter said, with a big grin on his face.

Bernice's car was coming up the driveway and pulled to a stop.

Bernice leaned out the open window and said, "Ma insisted we come over to say one more goodbye to you. So here we are."

Molly came running up to give me a huge hug. "This was just the best week ever. I'll miss you Lillia. Safe travels back home."

"I'll miss you too, and I'll think of you enjoying Rose Cottage," I said.

Grauntie snapped a photo of Walter and Annabelle together to put in her digital frame.

Walter said, "Nora, you mentioned wanting to visit the Biltmore house. If you ever plan on going there, look up Alan Gall and tell him hi from me. Say things worked out and show him that photograph. He'll know what you mean."

"Will do. Lillia, you love old houses. Ready for another road trip soon? I've heard the Biltmore Estate is amazing."

Grauntie knew me, I was always up for an adventure.

Another round of goodbye hugs and the three of us piled in Grauntie's car and headed down the drive.

At the end, between the stone piers, newly painted gates stood wide open. And as we pulled out onto the gravel road, I saw the name Meyer in bright gold letters on the mailbox.

ABOUT THE AUTHOR

Please visit my website and check out the photographs I used as inspiration for *Locked Doors,* the fourth book in the Pameroy Mystery Series. Read about plans for the next books in the series. My goal is to take Lillia and her Grauntie Nora to all fifty states!

www.pameroymystery.com

My website also contains links to my Facebook, Instagram, and Pinterest social media sites.

I look forward to hearing from readers! I'd love to receive photographs of you reading *Locked Doors* or visiting Wisconsin. How about from the top of observation tower on Rib Mountain?

Happy reading...

Brenda Felber

Brenda@brendafelber.com

www.brendafelber.com
brenda@brendafelber.com

ALSO BY BRENDA FELBER

Unsettled Things, A Pameroy Mystery in Kentucky

Watched Places, A Pameroy Mystery in Alabama

Haunted Hills, A Pameroy Mystery in South Dakota

Made in the
USA
Monee, IL